THE
REWILDERS

LINDSAY
LITTLESON

pokey

First published in 2022 by Pokey Hat

Pokey Hat is an imprint of Cranachan Publishing Limited

Copyright © Lindsay Littleson 2022

ISBN: 978-1-911279-93-8

eISBN: 978-1-911279-94-5

Cover and Interior Lynx Illustration © Shutterstock / Tatyana Komtsyan

Cover Scenery Illustration © Shutterstock / Inky Water

Cover Wolf Illustration © Julia Dreams

*To my daughter Sally, and
all of her NHS colleagues
who have given so much in
the last two years.*

*Thank you forever.
You are superstars. xx*

1

ESME

As the car bumped into another pothole, Esme breathed on the window and wrote I'M DEAD with her finger. In the front seat, Mum gripped the steering wheel, oblivious, too busy cursing.

"Can that eejit not stop at one of those passing places and let us through? Is ten miles an hour really a tractor's top speed?"

"I don't know, and I don't care. You might be in a hurry. I'm not." Esme watched condensation dribble down the glass, obscuring the words. "You do realise you're ruining my life?"

Mum mimed banging her head against the steering wheel. "Give over, Esme. Don't be such a drama queen."

"I'm being serious! Isobel will never speak to me again."

"Of course she will. Isobel's a sweetheart, and you two have been best friends since nursery."

Mum's tone was scratchy, as if Esme was the one being annoying. Continuing the argument was a waste of effort, but desperation had set in. "It's over. She won't want to be friends any more. She'll—" Esme couldn't finish the sentence, couldn't say it aloud. Mum had no idea of the consequences she could be unleashing. Being Isobel's friend was vital. Falling out with her was unthinkable.

Esme huffed on the glass again and drew a sad face, while the car bounced along the lane towards Gran's whitewashed cottage. They'd arrived. It was too late to stop this earth-shattering disaster.

Mum glanced in the car mirror. "Cheer up, Esme. Please."

The rage and frustration which had been building in Esme's chest, hot as lava, erupted. "Cheer up? You've got to be joking!"

"I phoned Isobel's mum, remember?" Mum unclipped her seatbelt, opened the car door. "I apologised profusely on your behalf and explained you couldn't go to Isobel's party because you were spending the September weekend at your grandmother's." She sighed. "Esme, I know how disappointed you are, but it's just one of those things."

Boiling with frustration, Esme dug her nails into her palms. It hurt, quite a lot.

Isobel's party was not *just one of those things*. There was going to be a DJ, a massive cake, and a chocolate fountain. Nothing as exciting had ever happened in their little Highland village and there was every likelihood that nothing this exciting would *ever* happen again. But the truth was, she could have dealt with the disappointment, if it had been anyone's party but Isobel's.

Her mum was standing in the drive, but Esme didn't move. She unrolled the car window, making one last attempt to convince her mum that this was a terrible plan.

"*Please*, Mum. This really isn't fair. You don't understand. If I don't go, Isobel—"

Her voice cracked, and more tears spilled. Her mother lost patience.

"Oh, give over, Esme. Grow up, for heaven's sake. Get out the car."

Defeated, Esme undid her seat belt, and reached for her rucksack, buckling it up, moving at the speed of a slug.

Isobel's mum might have told Esme's that missing the party wasn't a problem, but it *was* a massive problem for Isobel. Last night, she'd called Esme, straight after their mothers had spoken on the phone. "Your mum said you can't come, but I take it you're planning to catch a bus, or get a taxi, or grow wings and fly, or something?"

Dread had slithered like a snake in Esme's stomach, as she tried to explain why none of those options would work. "Gran lives in the middle of nowhere and there's no bus service. I already suggested a taxi to my mum, but she said no way am I travelling in a taxi on my own at night, at my age. Like it'll suddenly be safe when I'm older! Believe me, if I could sprout wings, I would."

"Your mum's in London. What she doesn't know won't hurt her." There had been an edge of impatience in Isobel's tone. "It'll be easy. If you don't have enough cash, 'borrow' money from your granny's purse. She's ancient. She won't even notice. Phone a taxi and sneak out. You can do this, kiddo."

If they'd been face-to-face, she'd have had to laugh, pretend that the idea of stealing from her grandmother didn't fill her with horror. Even on the phone, she'd given a silly fake giggle. "Ha, ha, ha. Gran notices everything, and anyway, the mobile phone reception is rubbish."

Before Isobel could come up with any more plans, she'd rushed on. "Isobel, I'm sorry. I can't come to your party and that's the end of it. Believe me, I'm gutted."

For a long, painful moment, Isobel hadn't replied and Esme had imagined her china-blue eyes widening in shock and disbelief. "You've got to be kidding! You're seriously not coming? You're my best friend, you HAVE to come."

"I can't. I'm sorry." Her thumb had hovered over the end call button, and with hindsight, it would have been better to stop the conversation right there.

"I can't believe you'd let me down like this. I really thought you were my friend." Isobel's voice had

4

sharpened, and Esme's stomach had tightened, dreading her next words, knowing they'd be designed to hurt. "By the way, your new haircut? I only said I liked it to be nice, cos Ava was sniggering behind your back. But to be totally truthful, it's *terrible*; it makes your ears stick out. Ava and me think you look like one of those garden gnomes. You know, the ones with the wee fishing rods. The ugly things that only old people like."

Isobel had ended the call, and Esme had turned, to stare at her reflection in her bedroom mirror, and she'd cringed at the sight of her ugly, snub-nosed, big-eared gnome-like self. And then, she'd burst into tears, knowing her life was over.

Mum leant in the window and tugged at her bag. "Esme, hurry up, will you! I've a plane to catch!"

Powered by hurt, Esme flung open the car door. She stomped up the path, her rucksack swinging in her hand like a slingshot about to be loosed. Not that she'd ever fling her rucksack. Her iPad was in there (not that it was going to be any use to her, as Gran's cottage had no wi-fi) as well as the other, less important stuff, like spare clothes, a toothbrush and comb.

At the exact moment they reached the steps, her grandmother opened the door. Not in her normal way. She didn't fling it wide. She didn't call her usual greeting:

Come in! Come in! My two favourite lassies!

Instead, the door opened a crack. Esme only knew

Gran was there because she could see one plump hand, fingers clutching the door, holding it fast. "You cannae come in!"

Esme frowned, puzzled.

Gran's voice was breathless, as if she'd been running. "Fi, I'll see you on Tuesday. Don't work too hard. Esme, leave your stuff at the door and nip roon the back to check on that daft dug."

The door slammed shut. Mum and Esme glanced at each other, before Esme remembered she was angry with her mother, and looked away.

"That's odd," said Mum. "I hope she's not getting a bit... you know... senile." Esme whipped round, give her mother a hard stare. "Don't say that."

Mum's cheeks flushed. "Sorry. Your granny has all her marbles and more. I bet Shug has sicked up on the carpet again. If she'd let us in, we could give her a hand."

Esme pulled a face. "No way am I cleaning up dog sick."

Mum leant against the rickety porch, ready for a wait. Beside her, Esme swung her rucksack to and fro, like a pendulum on an old-fashioned clock. There seemed no point in dragging the goodbyes out any longer, when Mum's mind was already made up.

"You'd better go, Mum. You've got a plane to catch. Gatwick, here you come."

Her mother sighed. "Yippee. Lucky me. Try to make the best of it, Esme. I know it's not how you'd choose to spend the long weekend, but we're lucky that she offered. Otherwise, I don't know what I'd have done."

Pretended to be sick, asked Dad to come back from the rigs for a few days, left me home alone.... Esme had already suggested these and more. After all, she was twelve, in first year at high school, plenty old enough to take care of herself. But Mum had shot all her ideas down in flames.

Her mother reached out, attempting a hug, but Esme stiffened and ducked out of the way.

"I'll see you on Tuesday. At 2pm. On the dot. Bye."

It was only as Esme reached the end of the narrow gap between the cottage and the lean-to, that guilt began to niggle at her stomach.

I should have hugged Mum, said a proper goodbye. What if there's a zombie invasion? What if her plane crashes into a mountain?

Panicking, Esme started running back up the path, but it was too late. Mum's car was turning on to the main road and as Esme watched, it disappeared from view.

Esme stood, heart thudding, then pulled out her phone and typed a message.

LOVE YOU. SEE YOU TUESDAY XXX

It didn't send. *No, no, no.* She pressed again and again, but nothing happened. Esme hurried to the junction and had to leap out of the path of a logging lorry thundering past. Standing on the grassy verge, she pressed the button, and as the text sent, her heart rate returned to normal.

Nothing will happen to Mum now. She'll be fine. I'll not be orphaned and doomed to a lifetime of sadness and guilt.

For a moment, that thought was all that mattered. But then others crept back, gloomy as fog. It was only Friday morning and she still had four days at her grandmother's house to get through. And unless she sneaked out the cottage and walked five miles to the village and back, Isobel's party was going to happen on Monday night without her. And when the holiday weekend was over, everything would be different at school. She'd be on the outside, and she'd never get back in.

Esme trudged towards the back of the cottage, where a gate barred her way. The gate was meant to prevent Shug the Dug from getting out and trying to befriend the sheep. But Shug wasn't throwing himself against it, overcome with happiness to see her. He wasn't there.

As Esme unlatched the gate, an uneasy feeling slid down her spine. No slobbering licks, no wet, muddy paws. It was weird. Where was he?

Shug may well have been the daftest dog in the history of dogs, but he was definitely the friendliest. Spending time with Shug was the one thing Esme had been looking forward to. When that thought crossed her mind, guilt stabbed her again, sharp as a pencil.

Sorry, Gran.

She loved her grandmother. Short visits with Mum were fine. But Gran was an old lady... sixty-eight on her last birthday. And she didn't even drive. The long weekend was going to be endless.

The gate creaked as she closed it behind her, but then... silence. Silence was worrying. Shug didn't do silence.

Maybe he's chewing on poisoned berries? What if he's chased the sheep and been shot?

Shug seemed convinced that the sheep could be charmed into being his best friends, if he kept barking and running round them in demented circles for long enough.

When Esme looked around, she saw a long rectangle of mossy grass, a scattering of dead leaves. So far, so normal.

But where's Shug? And *what's going on in the house?*

The first mystery was solved right away, when a bundle of moth-eaten fur cannonballed towards her, sending her flying.

"Shug! Where were you hiding, you big eejit?"

'Big eejit' wasn't an unfair description. Shug was a largish dog, about the size of a collie, but mixed with a hairier breed. Gran described Shug as 'handknitted' and she didn't mean it as a compliment. His coat was greyish white with ink-black splodges, his ears were ragged triangles, folded in at the ends, and his hairy muzzle was permanently mud-splattered. It often appeared as though Shug had mud for brains too, but his heart brimmed with love for all humans, and Esme in particular.

As Esme got to her feet, Shug bounced round her, his big furry paws smacking against her jacket and jeans, smearing both with dirt.

But he calmed down quicker than usual and raced towards the drystone wall at the back of the garden. Then he bounded back towards Esme, nudged the back of her legs with his head and ran across the grass again.

It's as if he wants me to follow him, she figured, and so she did, letting Shug lead the way across Gran's soggy grass, and over to the hut.

The door was lying open and Shug raced inside. Esme heard claws scrabbling on boards, and garden tools clattering to the floor.

"Stop it, Shug! You'll wreck the shed. What've you found? Is it a mouse, or—"

She grabbed the dog by his collar, and stood in the doorway, blinking in disbelief.

2

CALLUM

"Callum! Get yourself down here, you lazy lummox."

Callum sighed, and put his precious phone back in his rucksack, as gently as if he were tucking a baby into a cot. Sadie had bought him the phone for his birthday in July—it had been the first time in his life he'd been excited about opening a gift, because before he moved in with Sadie, he'd always been asked what he'd like by a social worker, so knew what he was getting in advance. With its excellent camera and range of useful apps, the phone was perfect for filming.

He looked down at the two scenes he'd created on the table: a longship of tiny Lego Vikings heading towards the West Coast of Scotland, and a miniature camp of sleeping Scottish soldiers. Between them, he'd placed a field of fake grass, dotted with green and purple thistles, made from the smallest blocks but not quite to scale. He was planning to add expletive heavy captions for when the Vikings trod on the spiky plants, alerting the Scots army that they were coming. *The Battle of Largs* was going to be amazing, his best film yet, if he ever got time to finish it.

He'd spent the whole term wishing for the long weekend to come, so he could focus on his animations, forgetting that while school would stop, all his other chores would still have to be done. And there were a thousand extra jobs to do, jobs that had been piling up since the summer, waiting for him to have a spare moment.

The shed door needs oiling. The fence needs repaired. A wheel's come off the barrow.

It was lucky he was good with his hands. It wasn't that Sadie wasn't practical. She knew exactly how to hammer in fence posts and help a struggling ewe deliver a lamb. She'd kept the croft going single-handed for years. But she was no longer capable of doing it all herself. She was getting older, and that frightened him, more than he was prepared to admit. If he woke in the night, because of the barn owl's screech or a high wind making the slates rattle, he'd lie awake, worrying about what would happen to him next, if anything happened to Sadie.

Because he knew fine well what would happen next. One of the social work team would turn up, Katie maybe, or Brian, if either of them was still around (the social workers seemed to move on as frequently as he did), and he'd be moved to another placement, and it would go spectacularly wrong. And after a few weeks, once he'd *let everybody down*, he'd be moved to another one—like a bizarre game of Pass the Parcel—and it would continue, getting worse and worse, until he was impossible to place. Without Sadie, he could end up like those lads he'd seen in a TV programme last week: angry, unhappy youths who'd been shunted from place to place until they were sixteen, couldn't cope on their own, and ended up sleeping rough and doing time in Young Offenders' Units. When the presenter announced, *care-leavers are grossly over-represented in the prison system*, Sadie had grabbed the remote and switched off the TV muttering: *maybe if everyone stopped calling those boys care-leavers, they might believe someone still cared.*

Callum had no intentions of ending up in jail. His long-term plan was to go to college, do an animation course, become a professional film maker. Sadie was all for it and had told him all he had to do was keep out of trouble and stick in at school. But that, in the understatement of the millennium, wasn't proving easy.

"Callum! Come on, lad! What's keeping you?"

He'd better go, or Sadie might come up and fetch him—might even suggest he tidy up the table and put the Lego away. Mind you, Sadie could have tidied it all away at any time in the last few weeks, while he was at school, and she never had, unlike his last foster mother, who'd been manically house-proud and wouldn't leave his stuff alone for two minutes. He'd felt sorry for the woman's two young kids, and had told her so. Well, to be totally honest, he'd yelled at her, which had gone down like the Titanic, and was how he'd ended up at Sadie's.

Hurtling down the stairs, two at a time, he crossed the hall in a couple of strides and reached the warmth of the croft's cosy kitchen. Sadie was perched on a stool, pulling on mud-caked wellies, while Nell, her devoted Border collie, watched, eyes bright and eager, tail sweeping the flagstones. Poor Nell was clearly looking forward to the prospect of a walk and was going to be gutted about being left behind.

"I'm ready. Let's go." Callum grinned at Sadie and gestured at his clean jeans and jumper. "Will I do? You told me to dress up."

"Aye, very funny." Sadie, who wore her usual outfit of an ancient checked bunnet and her favourite John Deere overalls, lifted a scarf from the peg and threw it at him. "I tellt you to *wrap* up. The weather's turning. It's getting chillier, even in daytime, and you'll be out in the open aw night."

Callum pulled a face. Hypothermia wasn't an appealing prospect. But an adventure into the unknown was exciting, even if he'd much rather be travelling alone.

"You'll need a hat too." Sadie took his hat from another peg and tossed it in his direction. Reluctantly, Callum put it on and Sadie gave him a thumbs-up.

"You look awfy smart. "I like that jumper."

"Well, you would. You knitted it."

"Aye, so I did." She ruffled his hair, pride shining in her eyes, although whether the pride was in his appearance or in her knitting skills, he couldn't tell.

The jumper was horrible, and like the hat and scarf, was knitted in jaggy grey wool, which made him scratch like he had fleas, but he was wearing it to please her. He could tell she was worried, not least about Jean's decision. Though probably not as worried as he was…

"Oh, crivvens! I nearly forgot your sandwiches."

Sadie rushed to the bread bin and pulled out an uncut loaf. She seemed to have read Callum's thoughts.

"It's daft of Jean to involve that lassie. You could have managed this job yourself, no bother." She waved her carving knife in the air like a weapon. "From what Jean's told me, the girl doesn't have the sense she was born with. Hairdos and manicures, and fancy-dancy clothes. Spoiled rotten, by the sound of it."

"Aye, I guess she is." Callum sat down on the stool by the range, and stroked Nell's soft fur. He said nothing more. If he told Sadie everything, she'd be up at the school office as soon as the holidays ended, demanding to see the Head Teacher, and threatening to run him over with her tractor, if he didn't get it sorted.

Sadie snorted louder than Morag, her treasured pot-bellied pig. She pulled cheese and butter from the fridge and slammed its door so hard the glass bottles rattled.

"And the lassie's best pals with that besom Isobel Renfrew, apparently, so she's no pal of mine. Don't think I didn't clock Isobel's carry on at last week's parents' evening."

She fell silent, and Callum's hand went still on Nell's fur. Parent's Evening had been awful. The pupils had been encouraged by the teachers to come along too, but he'd had to be dragged by Sadie. And it had been even worse than he'd imagined. At the beginning of their ten-minute chat, his English teacher Mrs Chalmers had insisted she was going to *focus on the positives* but there clearly hadn't been any, and she'd ended up criticising everything, from his *peculiar pencil grip* to his *challenging behaviour*. And then it had got worse, because when he and Sadie had been walking down the main corridor, Isobel and her mother had passed them, and Isobel had made out she was scared, grabbing her mum's arm and cringing against the wall. It was horrible.

As Sadie cut the sandwiches she'd made into halves, she started to speak, her voice so hoarse that she had to stop and clear her throat.

"When I clocked how Isobel carried on when she saw you, as if you were the Big Bad Wolf, I'll admit, I felt ashamed, and I was worried that there had been truth in aw those phone calls from the school about you being a bully."

Callum noticed her hands tremble as she wrapped

the sandwiches in tinfoil. "Sadie, I didn't…"

She placed the sandwiches on the table in front of him, and he saw tears glistening in her eyes. "I'm sorry, son. I'm really sorry, that I doubted you. When we were checking out your pictures in the art room, I caught that wee so-and-so smirking when her mum's back was turned, and I thought, *oh, that's how the land lies, is it*? Next time that heidie phones and tells me you've nicked something out that lassie's bag, I'll be getting him to double check his facts. I've the measure of that yin."

There was real venom in her voice, and Callum stopped lacing up his walking boots, and grinned. If only Sadie could sit beside him in class, his troubles would be over.

Sadie's eyes crinkled as she thought aloud. "Having said aw that about Esme not being any use, I'd be worried you'd get lonely out there on the moor, aw alone. And maybe it is a two-person job, right enough. Once you get to the estate, it could get hairy, wi aw those wild beasts."

She hobbled over to her bookshelf and pulled out one of her favourite books, a battered copy of *The Novels of Robert Louis Stevenson*. The book had tiny print, so small Sadie could no longer read it, even with her glasses, so in the evening, when they sat together in the living room after dinner, warmed by the crackling log fire, Callum often read aloud. At first, he'd hated the idea, but he'd actually enjoyed Stevenson's stories.

"You'd better take this, for the nights. You've packed spare batteries for the torch, I hope?"

Nodding, Callum started pulling on his jacket, a hooded parka that his social worker, Katie, had bought him, '*because you're going to be living in the frozen North*'.

"Just think, lad, you're going on a dangerous quest, like David Balfour in *Kidnapped*, or Jim Hawkins in *Treasure Island*!"

Sadie waved the book in the air and gave a rather witch-like cackle.

Callum laughed. "Sadie, believe me, Esme McKinnon would be my last choice of companion on a dangerous quest. There was a spider in the girls' toilets last week and you should have heard Esme and Isobel shrieking. They're total drama queens."

Sadie rolled her eyes. "Well, she'll meet plenty more spiders where she's going, so take earplugs! I don't know what Jean's thinking. The wummin's my best pal, but she can be as daft as that dug of hers. Och, look at the time. We need to get going." The old woman started muttering to herself. "Car keys, check. The boy, check…" She stopped and glared at him. "You've forgotten your rucksack, you wee numpty!"

"Oops, I'll go and get it."

"Did you pack clean socks and pants? You'll be away for three nights, maybe four. Don't want you coming home reeking."

"Yeah, but Sadie, I need to know exactly what to do when—"

She waggled a finger at him.

"I tellt you. It'll be awright on the night."

As Callum trudged back upstairs, his boots clattering on the wooden risers, dread began to seep into his bones.

Today, his home life was heading on a collision course with school, and he preferred to keep them well apart. If it wasn't for school, he'd be happy enough—reading by the fire, making Lego animations in his attic room, helping Sadie keep the little croft going. School was where it all went pear-shaped.

The local high school wasn't large. There were only fifty-two pupils in first year and almost all of them were going to Isobel Renfrew's party on Monday night. He was the only one not to have been invited, and while he pretended not to care, it hurt like a wasp's sting. Of course, he knew why he'd been left off the list. He was the Bad Boy, the Bully, the Troublemaker. The other pupils hated him, and he hated them.

As he came back downstairs, Sadie was in the hall, pulling a manky red anorak on top of her overalls. She zipped up the jacket, and then picked the Robert Louis Stevenson book up from the hall table. Callum grimaced. He'd been hoping she'd forget. That book was heavy, and they had a long way to go.

"That's the way, squeeze it in."

He did as he was told. The rucksack already weighed a ton, but he didn't want to hurt Sadie's feelings. Not when they were about to be saying goodbye to one another.

"Right, we need to get a move on. I tellt Jean we'd be there afore eleven, as the lassie's due on the hour. It'll be getting dark by half seven, so the sooner you set off the better."

She hobbled to the front door, leaning on her walking stick, jiggling the pick-up's keys in her other hand. "Come, Nell. Kennel for you, lass."

Obediently, the old dog limped towards the front door, head drooping sadly, understanding that she wasn't invited. Callum followed, his rucksack hooked over one shoulder, and gave Nell one last pat before he got into the pick-up.

As Sadie turned the key, and the engine throbbed into life, Callum felt a strange mix of emotions swirling in his stomach. Nerves, fear of the unknown, homesickness. He knew he'd miss the solid comfort of the croft. And he'd miss Sadie.

He'd given her a hellish time when he first arrived– stealing money, swearing, punching walls—but she hadn't once wavered, hadn't ever threatened to send him packing. She'd not accepted any nonsense, but he'd soon realised that beneath her brisk manner, Sadie had the kindest of hearts. And her cooking was a lot better than her knitting. For the first time in his life, he was getting opportunities to cook too, and often prepared dinner for the pair of them. Spaghetti carbonara was his speciality.

Sadie swung the pick-up out on to the road, and Callum gazed out the window at the squat, slate-roofed croft. Nell was standing forlornly by her kennel, ignoring the black-faced sheep grazing nearby. The croft felt like home, and until Callum had come here, he might as well have been homeless, he'd felt so unsettled, so utterly alone.

Not that Sadie had been his vision of the perfect foster placement. He'd had a completely different idea in his head: a wealthy professional couple with a smart town house and a fancy car, desperate for a son of their own, so desperate that they were happy to shower their foster child with expensive electronic gadgets, and were totally prepared to overlook the fact that Callum Docherty had five previous failed placements and had appeared in front of the Children's Panel on more than one occasion.

But, unsurprisingly, his imaginary perfect parents never turned up, probably distracted by some curly haired three-year-old with dimples and no previous convictions. Instead, Callum got Sadie and Sadie got him. He'd been staying with her since the spring, and it was September now, making this his longest placement yet. And his happiest, by far… if it wasn't for school.

As the battered vehicle rumbled along the single-track road that wound across the moorland, excitement started to fizz like sherbet in Callum's chest.

I'm heading on an adventure into the wild. I'm going to use the survival skills Sadie has taught me. I'll see wild animals I've only seen on telly.

The thrill dissolved, as another thought hit him.

I'm going to be spending three or four days in the company of Esme McKinnon. That's not going to go well.

For the rest of the journey, the injustices dealt to him at school swirled in his brain like poison gas. Before the summer, his primary teacher had insisted he should make a Father's Day card, and then given him a detention for swearing. At the beginning of this term, his first at high school, Mrs Chalmers had announced that they should create illustrated family trees for homework as a *'Getting to Know You'* activity. Sadie had dealt with that one, throwing the worksheet onto the Head Teacher's desk and announcing Callum would be doing the task over her cold, dead body. The incident had done nothing to improve his relationship with Mrs Chalmers. The teacher always believed Isobel, even when Isobel was clearly lying. And whatever lies Isobel was telling about him, Esme was there at her back, smirking, and agreeing with every word.

Esme McKinnon's presence was going to ruin everything.

3

ESME

Inside the hut, Esme could make out the outlines of two shadowy figures, sitting side by side, as though they were waiting for a bus, on the battered trunk in which her gran kept tools and other junk. For a split second, fear caught her by the throat.

Ghosts!

But there was no such thing as ghosts. She knew that. So, it had to be burglars, stealing Gran's tools, though why they'd want any of the junk in here was anyone's guess. Breathing hard, she used her free hand to grab a garden trowel from its hook and sliced the air with it.

"Get out!"

"Callum, what on earth's the lassie doing? Is she no the full shilling?"

"It's not the friendliest of welcomes, is it? At least the dog's pleased to see us."

Esme's heart plummeted into her brand-new, fur-lined boots. She knew that voice. And as her eyes adjusted to the dim light, she recognised the figures sitting next to the rusting wheelbarrow.

Oh, no. It's worse than ghosts. Worse than burglars! It's Sadie McIvor and Callum freaking Docherty. What are they doing, lurking in Gran's shed?

Again, Shug threw himself forward, barking excitedly, struggling hard to free himself from her grip.

"Stop it, Shug, you silly mutt!"

The dog ignored her, so she clung more tightly to his collar.

It's too dark in here. I need to be able to see them properly.

Esme dropped the trowel and glanced at the shed window. The glass was draped in sacking, because Esme's grandmother insisted on covering virtually everything in her home with pieces of cloth, from crocheted throws on the couch, to garishly patterned vinyl tablecloths on the kitchen table.

When Esme tugged the sacking with her free hand, it ripped, disturbing a tarantula-sized spider, who scuttled down the frame and across the floor. A thin stream of daylight spilled into the shed, making the dancing dust motes glitter like flecks of gold.

Esme looked up, ignoring the massive spider haring across the floorboards towards her, and faced the real threat: the woman in wellies and a filthy anorak and the tall, thin-faced boy. She glanced from one to another, feeling her insides shrivel, burnt by the anger in their accusing glares.

Shug launched himself forward, and almost dragged her off her feet; Esme let go of his collar. The dog's furry tail waved like a flag in a high wind, and knocked over a rake and a basket of apples.

"Hush, you daft dug." The woman's voice was croaky, as if she'd swallowed a frog.

There was no longer any need to be afraid. These two weren't strangers, but Esme's feet felt frozen to the floorboards, her brain screaming, *don't go any closer!!!*

Callum was staring straight at her, as cold and silent as snowfall, his eyes like chips of ice, making no effort to disguise his dislike. Esme opened her mouth to speak, but could think of nothing to say. Without Isobel, she felt vulnerable, like a baby hedgehog with soft spikes.

The old woman spoke again, in the same harsh tone. "You must be Esme. What's kept you?" When Esme didn't reply, she ploughed on. "I'm a friend of your gran's. Sadie McIvor, from Old Lang Croft. You know my Callum from school. He's told me aw about you."

The statement hung in the air. Esme tore her eyes away from the boy's glare and grabbed again at Shug's collar. Guilt was making her cheeks flush, and her chest tighten. She was regretting her recent haircut. Her hair had used to be waist-length, and its swinging curtain would have helped disguise her scarlet face. And she thought bitterly, with her long hair she'd looked less like a ginger gnome.

But why are they here? Callum must have told Sadie what happened at school and she's come to Gran's house to complain, but why not go to the front door like normal people? And why come here at all? It isn't my fault. If they want to moan about it, they should be round at Isobel's.

"Um, hello, Sadie. Hello, Callum. Shug, calm down!"

The dog was barking in delight, tail thumping the floorboards, overcome with joy about having the chance to welcome strangers. If there was a prize for World's Worst Guard Dog, Shug would win it.

Sadie McIvor shook her head. "I've tellt Jean a million times to get that dug to training classes." She lifted her walking stick, and pointed it at the dog, like a witch casting a spell.

"Be a good dug, an shut your mug."

Immediately, Shug stopped barking. When Esme let go of his collar, he lay down on the floor of the shed, head on his paws, looking up at Sadie with big, adoring eyes.

Esme's jaw dropped. "Wow. That was amazing. Shug never normally does as he's told. He's a bit dense."

The boy laughed, but there was no warmth in it, and his grey eyes remained cold as winter. "Thick as mince. The dog I mean, not you. Clearly not you."

Thick as mince.

Esme stiffened, as she remembered where she'd last heard that phrase.

Last week, when Mrs Chalmers had gone out of the

classroom for a minute to speak to the Head Teacher, Isobel had leant over Callum's desk and waved his spelling test in the air.

"OMG! You only got eleven out of twenty! Total loser. I knew you were dumb, but you're as thick as mince!"

Everyone had howled with laughter, except Callum, and Katrina Henderson. Esme had noticed Katrina redden, and place her hand over her own work. She'd remembered that Katrina had dyslexia—and wondered for a moment if Callum did too. But Esme had laughed along with the others. Isobel liked people to laugh at her jokes. If you didn't, you were likely to be the butt of the next one.

Esme's jacket felt uncomfortably warm and her skin prickled with sweat. "Does my gran know you're here? Because I really think—"

Sadie nudged Callum and sniggered. "Not so thick as all that. She can think. She said so herself!"

Esme blinked. *They're ganging up on me. It's me against them.*

It wasn't a pleasant feeling; it was scary, as if she'd been lured into a trap. She felt suddenly claustrophobic, and wanted to run outside, breathe in fresh air.

Taking a deep, calming breath, Esme spoke as firmly as she could. "Look, I don't know why you two are lurking in here, but I don't think my gran would be too pleased about it. You need to get out of her shed."

Sadie's eyes narrowed. "Oh, hark at that yin, giving orders. We'll do as we please, young lady. This isn't the playground. You're no wi the Queen Bee now."

The woman struggled to her feet, glaring at Esme. They were about the same height, but the physical resemblance ended there. Esme was freckle faced, green-eyed, with bright red hair cropped short. Sadie's skin was weather-beaten, etched with lines, and her hair grey and straggly, tied back under a mannish cap. The girl could feel the woman's anger radiating, a flame of rage, and shrank from it.

This isn't fair. I'm not to blame. If it had been my party, I wouldn't have invited Callum obviously, because nobody else would have come if I had. But even so, I'd have been a lot more tactful than Isobel about handing out the party invitations. I'd have done it discreetly, behind his back, not made a big song and dance about swanning into maths and placing an invitation on everyone's desk except Callum's, like Isobel had done. I wouldn't have been as mean as Isobel.

Esme cringed, remembering Isobel's sneering words.

"You're not invited Callum Docherty, because everyone hates you."

As she'd walked away from his desk, she'd turned, holding her nose in faked disgust.

"By the way, your clothes reek of pig poo. It's pure mingin."

It had been so deliberate, the way she'd pushed Callum into losing his temper, and then wailed to the maths teacher, crying actual tears.

"Callum swore at me, Mr McLean, and I was only giving out my birthday invitations!"

Guilt wormed like an eel in Esme's stomach. She'd backed Isobel up, pretended to Mr McLean the swearing had come out of the blue. But Isobel had started it. None of this was *her* fault.

"If this is about the party, it was nothing to do with me. Isobel didn't want—"

Sadie drew nearer. Her clothes smelled of woodsmoke. "What are you on about? We're no here for a ruddy party!"

The boy tugged at her sleeve.

"Leave it, Sadie. Esme's talking about something else. I don't think she knows what's going on. Jean can't have told her about what's happening later."

Sadie tutted.

"Well, it was Jean's idea to involve her, so I don't know why she hasn't told her. What's the daft besom thinking?"

Callum turned to Esme and gave her an odd half-smile.

"We were told to wait here, by your gran, until the coast was clear. I take it your mum has left? Apparently, she has to be kept in the dark. In case she worries."

He put his finger to the side of his nose and tapped it.

Esme opened her mouth and closed it again.

She has to be kept in the dark… in case she worries.

It sounded horribly ominous. What was Callum talking about?

She took another deep breath, but the calming effect didn't happen. She'd never felt so uncomfortable in her life, nor felt so *seen*.

"I'm stuck here at my gran's house. So, I'm not going to the party either, you know."

She might have known not to expect sympathy.

Callum shrugged. "I don't care about the stupid party, Esme. We're going to be working together. We don't have to get on. This isn't about us. It's about Cora, and it's about doing the right thing for the planet."

Callum's peculiar speech was having a startling effect on Sadie. As he spoke, tears started trickling down her reddened, wind-scoured cheeks.

"I'm going to miss the wee lass so much." She gave an enormous sniff and wiped her face on the sleeve of her dirty jacket.

Esme gawped at Callum, utterly baffled. "What the heck's going on? Who's Cora?"

But his expression was unreadable, his eyes as dark as smoke. He gave her that odd half-smile again. "You'll find out soon enough."

A clatter behind her made Esme jump and she whirled round.

"Here I am, sweetheart. Sorry I took so long!"

"Gran!" Esme almost burst with relief at the sight of her gran, standing in the shed doorway.

Something, however, wasn't quite right. Gran was wearing a nice pink fluffy cardigan, smart trousers and trainers, but there were white, downy feathers in her hair, and she had a long, bloody scratch down one cheek.

"Hello, Sadie, young Callum. Hope you've made yourselves comfy. Good to see you, Esme!"

As Gran wrapped her arms around Esme and squeezed her tight, the girl closed her eyes.

Everything's going to be okay. This is just a bad dream, brought on by guilt and the cheese sandwich I had for lunch yesterday.

But when she disentangled herself from her grandmother's arms, Sadie and Callum were still there.

Sadie gave a curt nod. "You've taken your time, Jean."

Gran ignored the snippy tone and smiled at Esme. "I take it this pair have explained it aw?"

Sadie clicked her tongue. "That was your job, no ours."

"I've hardly had time, have I? Not with the wee lass creating havoc."

Esme's heart was drumming against her ribs. *What wee lass? What's going on?*

Her grandmother took her hand. "Sadie and I have done something very stupid, Esme. And we need you, and the lad here, to fix it."

Esme stared at her, heart racing, trying to figure out a sensible reason for all this craziness.

Callum and me are kids. You're meant to be the grown-ups.

As if she'd heard her, Gran heaved a huge, sad sigh.

"We wouldn't ask you if we didn't think you could do it. We'll miss her, of course we will, but it's for the best."

She stepped forward, propelling Esme out of the shed, but then stopped dead. "She *has* been a terrible handful. But she's a wee cracker…"

Sadie made a sound like a trumpeting elephant. "Stop dithering, woman. Let's go and get this done."

They made an odd little procession, trailing across the lawn towards Gran's back door, the two women, Callum and Esme, accompanied by Shug, who stayed nicely to heel, but was so ecstatic to have company that he peed on the grass twice.

When they reached the back door, her grandmother put a warning finger to her lips.

"Caw canny. She's been a bit wound-up today. Shug, stay out. It's no safe in there wi aw the broken glass."

Warily, Esme entered the kitchen, and gasped at the mess. Normally, the kitchen existed in a happy state of comfortable untidiness, but this was a whole new level of squalor. Every cupboard door hung open, one swinging on broken hinges. Shattered glass gleamed in a dustpan by the bin. A cereal carton lay toppled on the floor, spilling bran flakes, which crunched under Esme's feet as she zig-zagged her way across the room, trying to avoid the shards of glass still glittering on the floor.

"Gran?" Her throat felt tight, and her brain was whirring.

Is my gran going senile after all? Is she being exploited by some wild teenager who has moved in and is trashing the house? And if the girl is this out of control, why did Gran say that she'll miss her?

"Gran?" she repeated. "What on earth is going on here?"

"My fault." Her grandmother sighed heavily. "I went outside to bring in the washing, and this happened. When I tried to shoo her out the kitchen, she wasn't happy." She pointed at the scratch on her face. "I haven't had time to sort the mess."

Sadie's eyes creased with annoyance. She shoved past Esme, stomping towards the hall. "You shouldn't have left her alone! I hope she hasn't been hurt."

Gran's eyes filled with tears.

"It's no like tending to a baby goat or a newborn lamb. This yin's as wild as… as wild as—Sadie, don't open that door!"

4

CALLUM

As he followed the two women into the hall, Callum's heart was racing. For days, he'd been anticipating the moment he finally got to meet Cora, and now that it had arrived, he had to fight the impulse to dart ahead, and push his way into the living room. He glanced round at Esme, wondering what she was making of this mystery, but she just looked dazed.

As Sadie reached the door, she turned and gave a heavy sigh.

"Och, Jean, I'm sorry, hen. I wasn't being fair. I ken how much work Cora has been recently and you've taken good care of her. Put the kettle on and I'll help you tidy up the mess in the kitchen. The bairns can introduce themselves to Cora."

"Aye, a wee cup of tea's a fine idea."

Harmony restored, Jean and Sadie retreated to the kitchen, leaving Esme and Callum standing at the living room door.

"Who the heck is Cora?" asked Esme again. Callum

didn't reply, partly because he wasn't a hundred percent sure himself. He hadn't seen Cora, only listened to Sadie's garbled tale of theft and arguments and panic. The two women might have got it all wrong. Some domestic cats, like the Maine Coon and the Norwegian Forest, were much bigger than the average. But what if Sadie was right?

Anticipation buzzing in every nerve, Callum turned the handle. The door swung open and he stepped inside. The first thing he noticed was the pungent, acrid smell of cat pee. His lip curled and he put his hand to his nose. "Oh, man. That's honking."

Behind him, Esme spoke, her voice tinged with horror. "What's happened here? What on earth's that horrible stink?"

Callum took a few cautious steps forward, nerves tingling. His heart was banging against his rib cage. He was desperate to see Cora, but he didn't want to be dinner—the information he'd googled yesterday in the school library had made him wary.

Skilled hunters, so quiet and secretive that their presence in an area could go unnoticed for years... they are excellent climbers and use rocks and trees to watch for prey to ambush.

So where was she lurking, and was she likely to pounce?

The room was in semi-darkness, as the wooden

shutters were drawn, but when Esme flicked the light switch, Callum gasped. The room was a shambles. A chair was upended, castors still spinning. Smotes of ash from the open fire swirled in the draught. Pictures hung on the walls at crazy angles. A ripped cushion lay on the floor, and its fluffy white feathers spun like snowflakes.

He saw the cat right away. In her natural environment, her reddish-brown fur would have been excellent camouflage, but the poor beast was unable to hide herself against a background of rose-sprigged wallpaper. In a corner of the room, beside a massive oak sideboard, she crouched: dark-spotted, long-legged and about the height of a Labrador.

"Wow..." he murmured, unable to take his eyes off the animal. The cat stared back at him, eyes like amber headlamps, long, tufted, triangular ears twitching. Her intelligent expression and fluffy white beard gave her the face of an ancient, wise guru, and it was hard to believe she was so young, only a few months old.

Beside him, Esme gasped. "Is that a... is that a lion?"

He'd promised himself he wouldn't speak to Esme any more than necessary, but couldn't help seeking revenge or stop himself mocking her ignorance.

"Don't be a numpty. It's a Northern Eurasian Lynx, of course. Everyone knows that."

Esme flushed scarlet as her hair, but he didn't care. Isobel had called him stupid often enough, and Esme had laughed every time. She'd stand there, at Isobel's side, grinning, full of herself, loving being one of Isobel's gang.

"It can't be." She shook her head, appearing to be unable to believe what she was seeing. "Lynx are wild animals."

He rolled his eyes. "So are lions. And giraffes. And hippopotamus. But this particular wild animal is a lynx."

As he spoke, Callum kept his eyes firmly on the cat. In the wild, Eurasian lynx were reclusive, and avoided humans completely, but they could be aggressive when cornered. The lynx stared back at him, and yawned, as if the sight of him bored her, revealing a gory, blood-red mouth and rows of needle-sharp teeth.

Esme's eyes widened and she took a step backwards. "Okay, so she's a lynx, but what's a lynx doing in my gran's house? Has she escaped from a zoo?"

The sound of Sadie's stick clicking on the hall tiles made Callum turn. She waved at him. "We thought we'd better come and check the wee devil's behaving herself!"

He watched his foster mother hobble down the hall, trying to keep ahead of Jean. There was no doubting how fond they were of Cora, but the two women had really messed up. Their behaviour hadn't shocked him, but how would Esme feel, about her grandmother being a criminal? A mischievous smile tugged at the corner of his mouth.

"You asked what the lynx is doing here?" He was looking at Esme, but raised his voice, so it carried. "Jean and Sadie stole her."

"We did no such thing!" Jean pushed past Sadie, who was standing in the doorway, surveying the mess. "We didn't steal her!" She put down the tea tray and flopped onto the couch, sending duck-down from the ripped cushions swirling round her head. "Oh, for heaven's sake, I'm like a snowman in a snow-globe. Let me get a cup of tea to calm my nerves, and then I'll explain."

She poured tea into mugs and then pointed towards the lynx, who was still crouched in the corner, watching them.

"Right, here's what happened. In the summer, Sadie and I were visiting the Rothiecraig estate. We went for a wee stroll and we found a tiny, mewling, scrap of a kitten, abandoned in the long grass at the side of a path. The poor wee soul might have died if we hadn't rescued her."

Sadie broke in, determined to give an honest account. "Aye, she looked like she'd been abandoned. We picked her up and gave her a cuddle, but we know now that we should have left her where she was. And we should have let the gamekeepers at the estate know we'd found her. If we'd known that she wasn't an ordinary moggy, we would have." She hesitated, and then pointed at Jean, shifting the blame. "Taking the kitten home was that yin's idea."

Jean blushed and didn't argue. "I've had an awfy problem with mice, and you know Shug. He's useless. Enjoys the company of the mice and is too lazy to mind them sharing his dinner. I thought the kitten was a stray, and nobody would mind. It was only as the weeks passed, and she started to get bigger… and bigger… that I realised I'd made an awfy mistake."

Sadie sank into an armchair and gave a heavy sigh.

"Aye, Jean called me, all discombobulated, and so I came roon here and took a few pictures of the cat. The following morning, I drove to the library, and asked Sheila, the wee lassie who works there part-time, for a shot of that internet thingy. Her jaw dropped, because, I'll admit, I've said my piece a few times about the library wasting money on computers when they should be spending it on books."

"You should have sent me instead." Callum grinned. "Sheila will think you're a right hypocrite now."

Sadie shrugged. "So what? As my maw always said, *'we've no say over what other folk think of us.'* We can only control what we do ourselves, so we should focus on that. Anyway, whatever Sheila's thoughts, she hid them well. In fact, the lassie was very helpful. She showed me how to get onto the Google." A triumphant grin spread across the woman's face. "It didn't take me more than a few seconds to find an animal that looked exactly like our Cora. Though finding oot the kitten Jean had taken home was actually a Northern Eurasian Lynx was a big shock to my system, I can tell you, and Jean didn't take it too well either."

"No, I didn't, right enough. I really thought Cora was an ordinary moggie, and she's no that." Jean appeared to be an expert at stating the obvious. "I mean, look at her. She's still a kitten and look at the chaos she's creating already."

Callum's mouth twitched, and he turned away, so Jean wouldn't think he was laughing at her.

"And she needs to go back, where she belongs, wi the rest of those big cats in Rothiecraig." Jean's voice cracked, and tears ran in rivulets down her wrinkled cheeks. "She needs to be free, and wild."

As if she'd been listening, the lynx left her position by the sideboard and started prowling, showing off her long body, and her short, black-tipped tail. Her paws were enormous, with big furry pads like snowshoes. As she passed Callum, she rubbed her shoulder against his leg, the way a cat might, and he felt the power of her muscles and the dense softness of her fur before she continued to pad across the carpet. She paced up as far as the television and back, in a well-worn path, stopping now and then to scratch at the wallpaper.

Jean's right. That animal needs to be free. She's miserable in captivity.

Esme was standing with her back against the wall, at

the far side of the room. She kept glancing towards the door, as if she was preparing to bolt.

"What if it attacks?"

"There hasn't ever been a case in Europe of a wild lynx attacking a human." Callum spoke confidently, but he couldn't be a hundred percent sure they were safe. After all, Cora wasn't living wild. She was trapped, and both animals and humans can react badly when they're cornered. That was one thing he knew all about.

"I don't understand." Esme's voice shook with nerves, and she couldn't seem to tear her eyes from the prowling lynx.

If it had been anyone else Callum would have felt sorry for her. Well, anyone else, bar Isobel.

"Gran, you said you got it from an estate? Where is this place and why do they have wild animals running loose? Isn't that really dangerous?"

"They're not running loose. At least they're not meant to be." Jean's voice was uncertain. "Cora was, mind you. We'd have known she was a lynx, if she'd been behind bars."

"The lynx are supposed to be behind high fences. Seven of them, four females and three males, have been released on Rothiecraig, an estate to the north of here," Callum explained. "The owner of the estate, Morag Campbell, is a massive fan of rewilding. She has reforested a massive area, but now has a problem with deer numbers. So, she has reintroduced a pack of grey wolves and the seven Eurasian lynx in an attempt to control the number of roe deer. In separate areas, of course, because in the wild, wolf packs have been known to take down a lynx."

"She has released a pack of wolves? Jeez." Under her freckles, Esme's skin had turned pale. "Remind me never to go for a walk anywhere near that estate."

Callum chewed on his lip, unsure how to break the bad news. "The problem is, Esme, that's what we're about to do. Thanks to Sadie and Jean here, one of the female lynx is missing a kitten. They need us to take Cora back to Rothiecraig."

Esme's eyes widened. "No way. That's not even funny." She turned to Jean. "Nan?"

But her grandmother didn't reply, just sat on her couch, picking feathers from her trousers. Panic started to flicker in Esme's eyes. "I'm not going anywhere near that place. No chance. Wolves scare me to death. It's not happening."

She turned to Sadie, who was sitting calmly among the debris, sipping tea from a mug. "It's your fault, as much as my gran's. Why can't you just bundle your stolen property into the back of your truck and take Cora back to where she belongs?"

Callum chewed on his lip, really struggling not to laugh now, as Sadie's face turned a vivid crimson.

She gave a deep, injured sigh. "Jean and I can't take her, because if we're caught on the estate, we'll be arrested, even if we're not with Cora."

Esme's eyes flicked from one woman to the other, clearly waiting for an explanation, but for a long moment neither of them spoke.

Then Sadie broke the silence. "We're not allowed on the Rothiecraig estate. We're banned. There might even be a legal injunction."

Callum had heard this saga already, but he couldn't stop his loud snort of laughter. Sadie glared at him. "It's no one bit funny." She clicked her teeth and told Esme the entire story. "Your granny and I went to the estate with the Woman's Rural. That snotty cow, Muriel Douglas decided our usual lunch in the village hall wasn't good enough, and arranged for us to go to Rothiecraig for afternoon tea."

Jean broke in. "Afternoon tea, have you ever heard of anything so daft! Aw it did was put me off my dinner."

Sadie rolled her eyes. "Jean, that was the least of your worries. Hold your wheesht and let me finish. So, after we'd eaten our sandwiches and scones, we aw split up and went for a stroll through the grounds. That's when we found the kitten. And after we got back from our walk, there was an unfortunate stramash between me and Ross Bauld, the estate manager. I was a bit uptight, you see, because we'd been standing in the rain, waiting for the coach to turn up. It was twenty minutes late, and I had the hens to see to."

Esme's gran snorted. "An unfortunate stramash? It was a full scale rammy!" The lynx approached the couch and sniffed her trouser leg. Slowly Jean reached out her hand and tickled the lynx behind the ears. "Aw, you're a bonnie lass, are you no?" She looked up again. "Aye, it was a complete rammy. Sadie shouted at Bauld that re-introducing wild animals was madness. She told him that lynx and wolves were vicious predators and if any of her precious sheep got eaten by one of his ruddy wild beasts, there would be trouble. There's been terrible stories in the papers, you ken, of escaped animals savaging sheep, so she wasn't completely out of order. But she probably shouldn't have threatened to use her shotgun."

"Och, be fair! I said I'd use the gun on Bauld, no on the lynx, or the wolves." Sadie seemed keen that Esme understand that point. "Wild animals can't help their natures. If they went after the sheep, they'd just be following their instincts. But that baldy-heided eejit shouldn't be setting wild animals loose on folk's farmland. He should ken better."

"Bauld by name, bald by nature!" Jean sniggered at the joke. "Anyway, Ross Bauld wasn't one bit pleased. He roared that people had no right to be spreading lies, and when Sadie had another go at him, he lost the rag, and tellt Muriel Douglas the Women's Rural wasn't welcome back on his estate. She was mortified, and raging wi the pair of us. It was a long, awkward journey home, I can tell you, and there's been a frosty atmosphere at aw the Woman's Rural meetings since."

Sadie's flush darkened to magenta. "Aye well, that's as maybe. But the point you missed, Jean—and when it comes to deciding who's to blame it's a crucial point—is that on that coach home, there was an extra passenger, one you'd neglected to tell me about. I didn't ken you had one of Morag Campbell's ruddy lynx tucked into your Co-op bag for life, did I?"

5

ESME

As the women's story unfolded, and as the lynx continued to pace, Esme's anxiety tightened its grip, until she felt her chest was clamped in a vice, her breathing constricted.

I can't stay here. I need to go home. This is a crazy situation. OMG, that big beast is coming closer. If it leaps on me, I'm dead. It'll grab me by the throat and crush my windpipe. That's what lions do, and there can't be that much difference. They're both big cats. They're both carnivores.

Panicking, she shrank back against the wall, as Cora prowled towards her, sniffing the air. When the animal's furry body brushed against her leg, Esme gasped. Her fingers tightened on the phone in her pocket. Reception was terrible here, but if she could get an emergency message through to her mother, surely Mum would rush back and rescue her daughter from this nightmare. However important the weekend conference, the prospect of her daughter being eaten alive would surely come first. Her fingers fumbled for the buttons, while she focused on her breathing, trying to calm herself down.

Wait a second, could all this be some kind of extended prank? Are Callum and Sadie making a fool of me, in revenge for Isobel's bullying at school?

But if so, why would her gran join in? There's no way Gran would be mean to her, whatever she'd been told by Sadie and Callum. The whole ridiculous story had to be true. Her grandmother had stolen a lynx.

But she didn't do it on purpose. When she'd picked up that kitten and stuffed it in her bag, she thought she was rescuing it. It was all a silly mistake. But that animal is wrecking her house. And it looks like I'm the only one around here with any common sense.

Esme let go of the phone. Mum would be on a plane by now. She could fix this herself. Cora was a problem that needed to be solved, and quickly. The sooner the problem was sorted, the sooner Callum and Sadie would get out of Gran's house.

She held up her hand and waved it to get their attention.

"There's an obvious solution, guys. If we construct a cage of some sort, and attach an apology note, explaining that the lynx had been taken by mistake, we could drive to the gates of the estate, leave it there. In the middle of the night, if necessary. That would work, wouldn't it?"

Jean grimaced and rolled up her sleeve, to reveal her bare arm, a mess of deep scratches. "We tried putting her in Shug's puppy cage. It didn't end well."

Sadie's mouth tightened. "It was a daft plan anyway. Our Cora shouldn't be in a cage."

Ignoring the pacing lynx, Jean heaved herself up from the couch and walked over to where Esme was standing. Her hug enveloped Esme, who felt some of the tension in her body melt.

It's going to be okay. She likes my plan. We'll get rid of the lynx, Callum and Sadie will go home and everything will go back to normal, just me and Nan.

In a very short space of time, the prospect of a normal day at Gran's house had gone from excruciatingly dull to very desirable.

"Sadie's right." Esme's gran gave her shoulders a gentle squeeze as Esme's spark of hope fizzled and died. "Cora has spent too long in captivity already. When the puppy cage plan didn't work, we thought long and hard, and we've made up our minds. With a little human help, Cora needs to be properly rewilded." She paused, her hands still gripping Esme's shoulders. "And we figure you two are perfect for the job."

As her sat back down, Esme glanced at Sadie, and caught her raising an eyebrow. She clearly didn't agree that Esme was capable, never mind as perfect as her precious Callum—maybe because Callum wasn't cowering against the wall.

He didn't seem one bit afraid. In fact, he seemed

perfectly happy about the whole idea. When he looked at her, there was a sneer in the curve of his lips, and a glint of amusement in his eyes. He'd known about the lynx, and he'd guessed she'd be afraid.

He thinks I'm a coward. And he's right, I am a coward. I've never stood up to Isobel in my life.

Esme straightened up, and moved away from the wall, still keeping a cautious eye on the big cat. She spoke quickly, so she didn't have time to think too hard about what she was saying.

"Okay, I'll do it. I'll go with Callum, and we can take Cora as far as the estate, but I'm not going over the fence and I'm definitely not going near any wolves. Cora will need to be on a collar and lead, so she doesn't chase sheep." She stopped, gratified to see that Callum was staring at her, open mouthed with surprise.

Cora yawned again, revealing teeth as sharp as a crocodile's, and Esme gulped.

"And she'll need to be muzzled so she can't bite," she added. "How far is this estate? If we set off now, will we be back in time for dinner?"

Callum laughed. "Aye, dinner on Monday night. The estate is about thirty miles away, and the plan is to take it slowly, to give Cora a chance to get used to the outside world. She needs to learn to cope in the wild."

"Monday night!" Esme did a quick calculation. "That's three nights sleeping in the open!"

Panic was ballooning in her chest. She had no idea how she was going to cope in the wild, never mind Cora. Again, Esme turned to her gran for help, but Gran was looking utterly unfazed by the prospect of her only granddaughter venturing off into the unknown, accompanied by a dangerous wild animal and the worst behaved boy in the school, and quite probably dying of exposure on a bleak Highland moor.

"It's mid-September, Gran. I'll freeze to death." Another angle occurred to her. Gran was supposed to be baby-sitting. "What will Mum say?"

"Well, obviously, she'd have a hairy fit if she knew, but she doesn't need to know, does she? And you won't freeze because Sadie and I have this expedition thoroughly prepared!" Gran's voice rang with pride, and was so loud Shug heard her, and started barking and scratching at the kitchen door, desperate to reach them. "We ordered the bivvy bags and the sleeping bags from a catalogue. The tents are top of the range. They'll withstand extreme weather and are very quick and easy to put up." Gran sounded as if she'd memorised *Which Tent?* magazine. "And the sleeping bags are goose-down, so you'll be warm as toast." She took a large slug of her tea. "We'll ron-day-voo outside the gates of the main house on Monday evening, once your mission's done. You'll both be desperate for a hot bath by then!"

Esme blinked and stared at her grandmother.

She surely couldn't be serious.

Callum spoke, and the mocking note had gone from his voice. "I know it's all a bit of a shock, Esme, and believe me, I'd be happy to go by myself, but your grandmother has been quite insistent that you should come too. I'm sure, though, if you really don't want to go, she won't try and make you."

There was a pitying tone to his voice, so irritating that Esme bristled.

"She doesn't need to make me. I already said I'd do it, didn't I?" She looked down at her bag, with its iPad, jumpers and jeans. "Though I might need a warmer jacket." Her gran beamed and Esme rolled her eyes. "Don't tell me. You've bought a jacket for me and it's top of the range. This blooming lynx has been one expensive mistake, Gran!"

Half an hour later, they were standing in the newly cleaned kitchen, ready to go. The bivvy bags and sleeping bags were lightweight, but even so, Esme felt she was being crushed by the weight of her brand-new rucksack, loaded with tins and packets of food, a water bottle, warm clothes, and even a compass, which she had no clue how to operate. Her head was swimming, dizzy with disbelief that she was actually about to embark on this crazy mission, leaving her precious phone and iPad behind, because as her gran had pointed out, they might get damaged and there was nowhere to recharge them. And there was no collar, no lead and definitely no muzzle for Cora.

"What if she runs off, and savages a sheep?"

Callum held up a lidded plastic box. "Hopefully, she won't. Sadie has given me her favourite snack: strips of dried meat, and I'll feed her little and often, so she'll stick around."

He opened the box and held up a stringy piece of dried meat. "You like rabbit, don't you, Cora?"

Cautiously, the lynx approached Callum, who dangled the meat in front of her, until she was a couple of metres away. When he threw it, Cora jumped up, jaws wide, and swallowed it whole.

Esme shuddered. "That meat smells truly disgusting."

"It's not for you, though, is it?" Callum snapped the lid of the box shut. "It's not always about you."

Sadie clicked her teeth. "It's time you two left. Daylight hours are getting shorter. Sunset's at seven thirty or thereabouts."

When Callum left the house, Cora by his side, and Sadie hobbling after them, Esme could hear Shug barking in the garden, delirious with excitement. Lugging her pack further onto her thin shoulders, she turned to her gran, who was wiping tears from her eyes. *But the tears aren't for me,* Esme thought bitterly. *She's not one bit worried about me. She's crying because she doesn't want to lose her beloved Cora.*

"I'll see you on Monday evening, best girl." Esme's gran pulled her into a hug. Her breath was warm against her ear. "I ken you think I'm being careless wi you, but it's the opposite. I think this could be really good for—"

Esme pulled away, too annoyed to hear any more.

"Really, Gran? You COULD just have said no when Mum asked. Are you sure you don't just want rid of me for a few days?"

Her grandmother gave her a stern look, determination in her set jaw. "That's a daft thing to say, Esme. Of course, I don't want rid of you. But this mission is in your best interests. And you'll agree by the end of it, I'm sure."

"No offence, Gran, but I doubt that very much. I said I'll go, so I will, but I'm doing it to help you. There's sod all in it for me. I hate camping. I hate Callum. I don't even like cats."

Esme was about to flounce out of the door, not the easiest of manoeuvres with a heavy rucksack on her back, but she hesitated on the step, not wanting to repeat the mistake she'd made with her mum this morning. "I'll see you on Monday night. Love you to bits. Look after Shug for me."

Her grandmother grinned. "Oh, did I no say? Shug's going wi you. He may not be the best of guard dogs, but he'll be good company for you on the journey." She must have seen doubt in Esme's eyes, because she kept talking. "Cora and Shug get on well enough. They tolerate each other, at least. So, no worries in that direction." Her gran leant forward and gave her a peck on the cheek. "Goodbye, best girl. Be brave."

Be brave. If only it was a quality she could switch on like a light. Esme stepped out into the garden and inhaled the sharp scent of pine from the nearby wood. Callum was waiting, his expression blank. As soon as he saw Esme approaching, he opened the back gate and started to stride across the moor, Shug bouncing along in front and the lynx padding behind, keeping close, sniffing the air, ears twitching. She moved as silently as a cloud, her mottled coat rendering her almost invisible against the dead bracken. Esme took up the rear, the rucksack heavy on her shoulders, her brand-new walking boots already nipping her toes. Seven or eight miles before stopping for the night suddenly seemed like a long, long way.

Esme sped up a little, determined to keep up with Callum, but he'd stopped already and was feeding Cora another snippet of dried meat from the box.

"She loves this meat, but it won't last long. We'll have to encourage her to practise her hunting skills."

"But isn't the whole point of the exercise to get her back to the other lynx, so her mum can teach her all that stuff?"

"That's the ideal, but there's no guarantee her mother will accept her, as so many weeks have passed. Young lynx usually stay with their mothers for up to two years, but Cora might have to cope alone. I hate to say it, but Sadie and Jean have really messed up here."

"Oh, poor Cora." Despite her nervousness round the lynx, Esme had a sudden urge to give the animal a comforting pat, wondering if Cora felt the same fear *she* had felt this morning at the very thought of being orphaned. Hardly able to believe she was doing it, she reached out a finger, touching the creamy, velvet-soft fur on the animal's chin and then hastily withdrew her hand, just in case. "That's such a shame for her."

She glanced at Callum, a horrible thought punching her in the gut. *Was Callum an orphan?* When they'd gossiped about him in class, Isobel had said he'd probably been so badly behaved at home that his parents had sent him to live with Sadie as some kind of punishment. But even as she'd laughed along, Esme had known that couldn't be true. Sadie was his foster carer, her gran had told her. She wasn't a blood relation. *Did Callum have no family of his own?* She was suddenly desperate to know, but there was no way she could ask. It was far too personal a question. She and Callum were never going to be friends. Not now, not after everything Isobel had done.

You can't blame Isobel for all of it.

The lynx's bright amber eyes were fixed on hers, and for a moment Esme felt the cat's gaze was accusing. She flicked the thought away like an irritating midge.

Instead, she wrinkled her nose, pointed at the box. "That dried meat does smell mingin though. Can we not persuade Cora to eat vegetables instead?"

"Lynx are carnivores, not herbivores. They're crepuscular carnivores. *Everyone* knows that."

Esme rolled her eyes. "Will you quit saying that. Some of us are too busy having social lives to watch boring nature documentaries." She'd have liked to know what *crepuscular* meant, but there was no way she was going to ask.

"Oh, I see. Are you still bitter about not getting to the party? Why don't you ask Sadie if she'll drop you at Isobel's on Monday night? I'm sure your pal will be thrilled to see you."

"Because I'll have unwashed hair and manky clothes. And anyway…"

She didn't finish. There was no point in trying to explain. Not to him, of all people. So, she trudged ahead, her boots sinking into the soggy ground. Shug trotted along beside her, his tongue lolling, tail wagging with happiness. At least someone enjoyed her company. Best thing to do was to ignore Callum, pretend he didn't exist. It was going to be a long, lonely, journey.

The wind whistled across the moor, ruffling her hair, freezing her ears and making her eyes nip. Far in the distance, jagged mountains loomed. She could imagine wolves roaming in these mountains, howling at the moon, hunting for prey. She could imagine running, terrified, across the rocky slopes, pursued by a baying pack, slavering at her heels, and she could only hope it wasn't a premonition of things to come.

6

CALLUM

They'd only been walking for two hours, and the pace was slow. Because Callum wanted to give Cora the chance to explore her surroundings, they'd covered less than five miles. But he was getting hungry, and guessed Esme was too. He waited until they reached a heap of lichen-roughened rocks, jutting like gravestones out of the damp grass, and pointed them out.

"Do you want to stop here for some lunch?" he asked. "These rocks look dry enough to sit on. I've a flask of soup and Sadie made some cheese sandwiches."

Esme nodded, tugged her backpack off her shoulders with a pained groan, and flopped on to a rock. When she pulled off her walking boot and sock, he saw that a blister was forming on her heel, so he took out the first aid kit, and passed her a plaster.

"Thanks. It's these new boots. Normally, I'd have walked about in them for a while, before I set off on a polar expedition."

Esme said nothing more, just focused on putting on

the plaster. When she pulled on her boot, he noticed her grimace. She'd been very quiet for the last two hours, completely unlike her usual loud, confident self. Or maybe, he thought, the girl he knew at school wasn't the real Esme at all. Maybe she behaved differently there, just as he did. What had Mrs Chalmers said about him... *Prickly, defiant, quick to anger*. That wasn't him. Not really. That was how he was at school. The spikes were his armour, Sadie said. Maybe Esme wore armour too.

He rummaged again in his backpack and found the greaseproof wrapped package. Unwrapping it, he held out a sandwich, like a peace-offering.

Esme pulled a face. "That bread has seeds. I don't like seeds. What sort of cheese is that? I only eat mild cheddar."

Or maybe Esme is the same pain in the neck wherever she goes.

"Sadie made them. I didn't check the ruddy ingredients." He didn't even try to keep the annoyance from his voice as he waved the sandwich under her nose. "Like it or lump it, but you'll soon starve if you're going to be fussy."

Esme took it, though she eyed the contents suspiciously and nibbled at the bread's edges, like a mouse with a nut. He found the dainty nibbling so irritating that he looked away and watched the lynx instead.

Cora was stalking imaginary prey; her body almost

touching the ground, her speckled coat merging with the undergrowth, her eyes fixed on a spot ahead. Callum saw her muscles tense, ready to spring, and he held tight to Shug's collar, worried the dog might interfere. Because he'd noticed the grouse, half hidden, huddled in the bracken. Cora's prey wasn't imaginary at all. She was hunting, behaving like a wild lynx for the first time in her short life.

Startled, the bird flapped its wings and soared into the air. Cora jumped, paws scrabbling. Unfortunately, the grouse flew higher, beyond her reach, and Cora thudded to the ground, a slightly embarrassed expression on her furry face.

"Wow, that was close," said Esme. "You go, girl. With a bit of practice, you might be able to cope in the wild, after all."

Callum glanced at Esme, surprised. After the comment about the smell of the dried meat, and the fuss she'd made about the spider in the toilets, he'd half-expected her to freak out.

"What are you giving me that look for? We've got to praise her when she does her best, don't we? It's like when Shug was a puppy and occasionally remembered to pee outside and not on the carpets. Lots of praise works."

"Tell that to Mrs Chalmers, will you?" Callum replied. The words came out, before he could bite them back, and he regretted them immediately, as he'd already decided that if he and Esme managed to avoid discussing school at all, perhaps they could get through this trip without any drama. And now he'd gone and mentioned school.

"Look, I've been thinking." He took a slug from his water bottle, as his mouth had gone dry. "You know how during the First World War, the German and British troops were fighting in the trenches, and then on Christmas Day, they had a truce and played football instead? I thought maybe you and I could do that."

"Yeah, that would be good. I'm brilliant at football." She smiled, a gleam of mischief in her eyes. "Just kidding. I get what you're saying. You mean, we should lay down our weapons for as long as this mission takes? Pretend to be friends?"

He grinned. "We don't need to go that far. But yeah, a truce. Keep school out of it. Focus on getting Cora home. After the holiday weekend, war can resume."

She turned away from him, but not before he'd seen her face cloud.

"Okay. Agreed. Let's get going. It looks like it might rain."

She wasn't wrong. Dark clouds were scudding across the distant mountains, and a smirr of moisture dampened the air.

Setting up camp in the pouring rain would be a misery and getting their equipment soaked would be stupid. But they hadn't travelled far enough. He'd planned to do at least seven miles the first day and they had hours of daylight yet.

"We'll stop when we get to Glen Craig," he said, heaving his backpack on to his shoulders. "We can refill the bottles in the burn below the waterfall, Sadie says. There's an area of flat ground there, and I reckon we can beat the rain, so it should be dry enough to pitch the tents."

"Sounds like you and Sadie had this mission all planned out." There was a bitter note in Esme's voice. "It would have been nice if someone had let me know earlier. I'd like to have been a bit more prepared."

They were walking side by side, both slightly hunched by the weight of their backpacks. The lynx was sniffing at Callum's heels, looking for more dried meat. Shug bounded over the soggy grass, tongue out, joy personified.

"So, if I'd marched up to you at school this week, and suggested we go on a camping trip, you'd have been up for it?" Callum failed to keep the mocking tone from his voice, despite his best intentions.

"Ha, ruddy, ha. But maybe Gran could have phoned and given me some advance warning. It all came out the blue and I think I'm still in shock. I certainly never had my gran down as a thief. Shug, come back, you daft dog!"

But Shug was off. The dog was heading towards a distant figure, a hiker maybe, who was heading across the moor, and who must have spotted them, because he seemed to be coming in their direction.

"Oh, for heaven's sake. Shug's gone off to talk to a stranger. Why on earth did your gran insist we bring that stupid mutt? He's going to cause problems wherever we go. Wonder what that guy's doing out here?"

There was no hesitation in Esme's voice. "Whoever he is, he mustn't see Cora. I'll stay here with her. You go and get Shug."

Slipping his backpack from his shoulders, Callum started running after the dog, cursing it under his breath. Shug kept on going, bounding towards the stranger. As Callum got nearer, he saw that the guy was holding a gun, and was pointing it straight at Shug. His heart hammering a hole in his chest, Callum yelled at the top of his voice.

"Don't shoot! The dog's with me!"

To his relief, the guy lowered the gun, just as Shug reached him and started leaping up, paws scrabbling, tail waving, totally oblivious to the danger he'd been in. As Callum ran up, and grabbed Shug's collar, the other person faced up to him, an aggressive scowl on his face. He was only a few years older than Callum, but much taller and broader. Even if the lad hadn't been armed, Callum wouldn't have fancied getting in a fight with him.

"You need to keep your dug under control! Keep it away from the sheep."

"Sorry, we didn't know." Callum paused. He didn't particularly feel like being friendly, but figured if the boy knew he lived locally, he might be less likely to shoot the dog if he came across it again. "I stay with Sadie McIvor, at—"

"Aye, I ken who she is. Sold my grandfather six ewes last spring. One of them's over there." Using the butt of his rifle as a pointer, the boy gestured towards a grassy hillock.

Shug was squirming to get away, desperate to smother this new acquaintance in affection, and Callum hissed at the dog, while he clipped on his lead. "Calm down, you stupid beast. The guy's got a freaking shotgun."

The boy shook his head. "It's an air rifle, no a shotgun. It's my grandfather's, but I've got a certificate, so I'm legally allowed to use it."

"On tin cans, maybe. You shouldn't be waving it at people's pets."

"Have you seen the damage a dug can do to a sheep? Come and take a look at this. Not that I'm blaming your dug. This was done last night, and I'm pretty sure I ken what's responsible."

Callum really didn't want to know what damage a dog could do to a sheep, and his boots felt heavy as he held tight to Shug's lead and followed the boy, over the hillock, onto a boggy patch of ground.

"My name's Luka, by the way. Luka Rydeski." He

pointed, at what looked like a pile of bloodied rags. "There she is. Poor beast."

Callum edged closer. The sheep's corpse was a gruesome sight: grimy fleece bloodstained and tattered, throat torn open, one eye pecked out by crows.

Shug whined, and Callum used his free hand to give the dog a comforting pat. "That's… horrible. So, you think a dog did that?"

Luka shook his head. "Not a dog. I reckon it was the wolves." The boy's face was tight with anger. "It's that daft wummin Morag Campbell, and Ross Bauld, her estate manager, and their stupid ideas, letting wild animals roam loose on the estate."

Callum gulped, and hoped the lynx didn't appear at their side. "The wild animals… they're behind fences, surely?"

"Well, if they are, the fences aren't doing their job. This isn't the first time a sheep has been savaged in these parts recently, and we all know who's responsible. My grandfather's spitting teeth, he's so angry."

Callum recalled Jean's description of Sadie's 'rammy' with Ross Bauld.

She bawled at him that lynx and wolves were vicious predators and if any of her precious sheep got eaten by one of his ruddy wild beasts, there would be trouble.

Callum wondered whether Sadie kept quieter now, whenever the subject came up locally, and he chose not to engage either, just focused on scratching behind Shug's ears. The dog leaned against him, butting his fluffy head against Callum's leg, seeming keen to leave.

"Look, I need to get back to my... friend." Callum gestured, deliberately vague. "We're camping out for a few nights."

"If you're out here after dark, you'd better be careful. Wolves are cunning, vicious killers, and they hunt in packs. You'd have no chance if they attacked."

Without another word, Luka raised his rifle, aimed and fired at a rabbit lolloping in the bracken. A high-pitched shriek shredded the air. Shug cowered behind Callum, his body trembling with fear.

"It's okay, boy. You're okay." He bent down and stroked the dog's ears, while glaring at Luka, angry that he'd given Shug such a fright. "There was no need for that. Look at the poor dog! He's petrified."

Luka shrugged. "He needs to toughen up a bit." He pointed towards the clump of bracken. "That was a good, clean shot. Looks like Grandpa and me are having rabbit for dinner."

Callum's thoughts flew to Cora's meagre rations, but he could hardly ask the boy for the rabbit. And he should never have read *Watership Down*, because it had made him squeamish about the very idea of killing them, much to Sadie's annoyance.

Only last week, she'd placed a brace of rabbits on

the kitchen table and rolled her eyes at the disgust on Callum's face.

"If we were meant to be herbivores, we wouldn't have been born wi these teeth, would we?" she'd grumbled, flicking at her canines. "You can get rid of that cat's bum mouth, or I'll make you help me skin them."

He'd scarpered up to his room, leaving Fiver and Hazel lying dead on the table.

And he scarpered now, saying a quick goodbye to Luka, and heading back across the moor to where he'd left Esme and Cora. Shug was now desperate to get away from this noisy, alarming stranger, and almost pulled Callum's arm out its socket as he raced across the heather to where Esme was sitting on a rock, hood up and shoulders hunched, a picture of misery.

When she saw them coming she stood up, and Callum was surprised to see tears in her eyes and fear etched on her face, until he realised she must have heard the rifle shot.

"What was that bang? I thought Shug had been shot!" Crouching low, she flung her arms round the dog's neck, and cuddled him, while Shug licked away tears. After a while, she let the dog go, stood up and faced Callum.

"You were gone for ages! I had to feed Cora some of the scraps, to stop her wandering off. I don't know how we're going to stop her heading off on her own. This is a crazy idea." There was an edge of panic in Esme's voice, and he knew he was about to make things worse.

When he'd finished telling her about the lad with the gun and the savaged sheep, her eyes were round as moons. "I know the Rydeskis. We should go back. We can't camp out in this wilderness when there are wolves around."

Callum shrugged. "You can go home if you want. I'm carrying on. For one thing, I don't believe wolves killed that sheep. Surely a pack of wolves would have torn their prey to bits, eaten it up. Not left the corpse lying on the grass, like a warning? And if Rothiecraig's wolves *had* escaped, it would have been all over the news, and there would be people out hunting for them. There's something odd going on, and I'd quite like to get to the bottom of it."

"Give over, Sherlock." Esme rolled her eyes. "I don't care what's going on. I just want to get Cora back to Rothiecraig and get home to my own comfy bed."

Callum nodded but didn't say any more. It sounded as though Esme planned to stick this out, and not run home, and he wondered if she'd believed what he had just said about the wolves, because he wasn't sure if he believed it himself.

By the time they reached the mountains that surrounded the pass into Glen Craig, the rain-clouds had dispersed, but the air felt damp and chilly. The waterfall was an easy landmark to spot, spilling from a rocky outcrop into the river that wound through the glen. When Callum went too close, the wind blew spray into his face.

When he looked up at the looming mountains, he felt a twinge of anxiety.

What if wolves are roaming free in these mountains? What if Luka's right?

He jumped, startled, as Cora padded past, on silent, over-sized paws. Cautiously, she approached the waterfall. Her tongue lapped daintily at the flowing water, like a domestic cat drinking from a kitchen tap.

Callum gave himself a shake. He had to focus on the important thing: getting Cora to a place of safety.

He called over to Esme, who had been trailing behind. "We can pitch the tents here, close to the water."

The tiny tents were easy to erect, and they managed without problems, although lighting a fire was a different story. When the little pile of damp kindling finally flickered into life, they both cheered, but when he looked up from the fire, grinning, Esme didn't look happy, just awkward and uncomfortable.

"I can't believe I actually cheered there." Esme rummaged in her bag and pulled out a can of spaghetti. "What a loser."

"You know, it's fine to be enthusiastic about stuff that makes you happy." He saw her roll her eyes, but he carried on. "If anyone laughs at you, that's their problem." As soon as the words were out his mouth, he cringed, realising he was being a massive hypocrite.

Yeah, so why don't I tell everyone at school I love building with Lego and reading classic books? Because I don't want them to laugh at me, that's why.

Luckily, Esme changed the subject. "Look at Cora! She's coming over."

Moving slowly out of the thick undergrowth beside the burn, the lynx approached, the firelight's glow reflected in her eyes. She sniffed the air, and then lay down close to the fire's warmth, almost within touching distance of Esme.

Callum watched in astonishment, as the girl edged a little closer, reached out a hand and gently scratched the lynx under the chin. Seeming to enjoy the scratch, Cora raised her head, showing off her rich, creamy ruff.

"I thought she'd be afraid of the fire," Esme whispered, a smile lighting her face. "I thought she'd be scared of me."

Callum sighed. "She *should* be afraid of fire. She *should* be afraid of people."

Esme's smile faded. "But isn't it lovely that she trusts us enough to want to sit close to us? And look how she likes getting her chin scratched!"

"Until she's scared of humans, she won't be safe in the wild. Perhaps we'll need to scare her really badly, so she won't stick around anymore."

It wasn't a happy thought, and it lowered his mood.

He'd been stirring the spaghetti with a stick, but it was bubbling, orange and wormy as a witch's potion, so he pulled the pan away from the heat of the fire. "Dinner time. And when it's finished, I'm heading for bed. We've got a long walk tomorrow."

When he'd zipped up the tent, and crawled inside his sleeping bag, pulling it up high so only his forehead was visible, he sighed happily. When he'd sat close, the campfire's flames had warmed his skin, but this was the first time since they'd set out that he felt truly cosy, warm inside and out, like a freshly baked loaf. Sadie and Jean had chosen the equipment well. Esme would be even cosier, with Shug draped across her feet.

As for the lynx, Cora seemed content enough to snooze in a den of crushed bracken and dead leaves.

But we're already running out of food for her. We'll need to find a way of feeding her, or she'll run off, and out on the open moorland, she'll be in terrible danger. If she's spotted by that boy with the air rifle, he'll be convinced she's the one who killed his sheep, and he'll shoot her on sight.

It took Callum a long time to drift into an uneasy sleep, until eerie howling split the night's quiet and he woke again, and lay, huddled in his tiny tent, knowing the flimsy material was no protection against the pack of wolves roaming the moorland.

7

ESME

As Esme rolled up her tent, she glanced over at Callum. There were shadows under his eyes, dark as bruises, and as he fried bacon over their campfire, he kept yawning.

"You look shattered. Didn't you sleep well?"

"Not great. You?" As Callum spoke, he tipped a bacon rasher onto a slice of bread, folded the bread and passed it to her, unsmiling.

"Thanks." She felt slightly unnerved by the anxious, uneasy expression on Callum's face, and tried to lighten the atmosphere. "I slept okay, though the ground was hard as rock, and Shug kept farting, didn't you, monster?"

The bacon smelled delicious, and she went to bite into the sandwich, her mouth watering. But then she spotted the bacon fat, thick and slimy, and her nose wrinkled in disgust. "Gross."

Tugging the rind from the rasher, she threw it on to the embers, where it sizzled, and curled like a stringy white worm.

Callum's voice was sour with annoyance. "You could

have given that to Shug. He wouldn't have turned up his nose."

At the mention of his name, Shug wagged his tail, whisking the sandwich out of Esme's hand and on to the grass. Callum sighed, and Esme felt her cheeks flame.

He'll think I dropped that on purpose.

The dog was gazing up at her, liquid brown eyes pleading.

"You have it, Shug. It's probably covered in beasties now anyway." She rummaged in her bag, pulling jumpers and socks out of the way to reach the bottom. "I think there are some cereal bars in my backpack. I'll eat one of those instead."

As she unwrapped the cereal bar, she was uncomfortably aware of Callum's disapproving expression.

"We can't waste rations," he snapped. "There isn't much food left, you know. We've a choice of tinned beans, soup or spaghetti and half a loaf of increasingly stale bread."

"Great. So glad I came on this trip, with its first-class food and facilities. Not."

"Yeah, well, the trip would be a lot easier for me if I didn't have to listen to your constant whinging."

When Callum had given Cora a few strips of dried meat, he and Esme finished packing away the equipment in stony silence and started walking the second section of their journey, from the Glen Craig pass to Ailcroft, a ruined farmhouse in the middle of the glen. At almost nine miles, it was the longest section and Esme hoped desperately that a lunch stop had been included in the itinerary, because the cereal bar had been dry and tasteless, and already her stomach was rumbling. But she didn't like to say, stung by his comment about her *constant whinging.*

Callum's face was thunderous, his eyebrows knotted, mouth a hard line. This was the version of Callum she knew from school, the sullen, silent boy the other kids avoided. The boy Isobel liked to wind up, then stand back and watch the fall-out.

It was a perfect September day, bright and sunny, the glen sheltered by the mountains from the worst of the wind. A wide burn burbled over rocks, winding its way through the glen, and the gurgle of running water and the twittering of the siskins in the pine trees, panicked by Cora's approach, were the only sounds.

Esme breathed in the clean, pine-scented air, enjoyed the warmth of the sun on her skin. Callum slowed his pace, and when she glanced at him, she saw that the tension had left his face, and he looked almost happy. Shug was in his element, running in circles, herding them together, then bounding off, distracted by a butterfly or bird.

"I came here with Sadie, during the summer holidays,"

Callum said, breaking the silence between them at last. "We fished in the river, though we only caught a plastic carrier bag. It was a warm, overcast day and the midges were hellish." He pulled a face, then gave her a rueful smile. "I told Sadie I wasn't ever coming back."

"At least the midges are staying away, and anyway, we've got repellent and midge hoods and goodness knows what else." Esme pointed at her bulging rucksack, the straps of which were already digging into her shoulders. "We're prepared for just about anything, except attack by wolves!"

The smile slipped from Callum's face. He gave her an odd, sideways look.

"Did you hear any noises in the night?" he asked. "Owls hooting, or anything like that?"

Esme shook her head. "I was zonked out. Shug's fart was the last thing I heard." She glanced at him, anxiety knotting her stomach. "Why are you asking? Did you hear something?"

"Nope. Only the wind in the trees and somebody farting. Least I know now it was Shug and not you."

She attempted a sharp poke with her elbow, and he laughed and dodged out of the way, while Shug, intrigued by the mention of his name, stopped sniffing at deer scat, and came bouncing over.

As they walked on, over spongy moss and springy heather, the atmosphere between them felt more relaxed.

But Esme hadn't been completely convinced by Callum's reply.

As soon as I mentioned wolves, he asked me if I'd heard noises in the night. Either he's trying to scare me, or he heard a wolf in the night, and he's the one who is scared.

Neither alternative was comforting, and it was a relief when they stopped for lunch and could focus on gathering firewood, on feeding Cora, and on setting the fire to boil water for Pot Noodles and tea.

The unexpected roar of an engine made Esme jump, and she almost choked on her mouthful of noodles. Both she and Callum leapt up, nervous as deer, as a quad bike bounced over rocks and heather towards them.

When Esme saw the gun strapped to the bike rider's back, her immediate thought was for Shug, but Callum had already slipped on the dog's lead. Esme snatched it out of his hand and held tight.

"Luka Rydeski," murmured Callum, but she'd already recognised him. Tall and broad shouldered, in a battered leather jacket and faded jeans, his air rifle slung across his back, Luka looked older than his sixteen years. It was only when he swore, and raised his gun, that Esme realised Cora was his target.

"No!" she screamed. "No, don't hurt her!"

But Luka wasn't listening. His finger was pressing down on the trigger. He was going to fire. Without hesitation, Callum threw himself at him, knocking him sideways. The air rifle fired, the pellet zinging through the air, scattering leaves on a nearby tree.

Terrified, Cora fled, bolting for a clump of pine trees. Shug too, yelped in fear. Luka scrambled to his feet, face contorted with anger, fists raised, but Esme leapt in front of Callum, dragging Shug with her.

"What are you doing, you stupid eejit!" she bawled. "Look what you've done, you total numpty! You've terrified the dog and you've scared away Cora!"

Luka's expression was caught between anger and astonishment. "What am *I* doing? Should I not be asking you two that? Was that a freaking lynx?"

"Yes, it was a lynx." Callum's voice was cold with fury. "And it was nearly a dead lynx. Esme's right, you're a total numpty."

"What the heck is a lynx doing in Glen Craig? Has it escaped from the estate?" Suspicion gathered like clouds in Luka's eyes. "Did that lynx kill the ewe? More of our sheep have vanished, you know. That's why I'm here. Looking for our missing beasts."

"We don't know anything about your missing sheep. It has nothing to do with our lynx. She's less than six months old and can't hunt. She's dependant on humans for food." Callum ran both hands through his hair, then let them drop to his sides. Esme noticed his fingers were twitching and wondered if he was desperate to grab the rifle from Luka.

She hoped he realised it was a terrible idea.

"Luka, I shouldn't have called you names. You're worried about your sheep, and I don't blame you." She nodded towards their campfire. "Why don't you sit down by the fire and we'll explain about Cora?"

Callum blinked, but then nodded. "Yeah, we'll make you a cup of tea and tell you the story."

"A true story," added Esme. "About two old ladies who made a terrible mistake."

Luka didn't take them up on their offer of tea, and he didn't sit down either, but he laid the rifle down, and leant against a tree, arms folded. "Okay, I'm listening."

They told him about Cora, and about what they'd been planning to do, until the lynx had been scared away, putting her life in serious danger

"This isn't my fault,' said Luka, his voice defensive. "And it isn't Sadie McIvor's fault either. Morag Campbell and Ross Bauld are the eejits—they're the ones wi the wild animals on their estate." Luka almost spat Campbell's name, his lip curling in disgust. "Escapes were bound to happen. But you're right. The lynx can't stay out here. She'll learn to hunt, when she must or starve, and then our livestock will be in danger. So, you need to get her back to Rothiecraig by Monday evening, or I'll be after her. And I won't miss next time."

"We'll take her home." Callum sounded confident, leaving no room for doubt, and Esme nodded in agreement, though she didn't think she'd ever been less sure of anything in her life.

Cora has run off, and no wonder. What if she doesn't come back?

The glen seemed an excellent place for the lynx to hide, protected from the worst of the elements, her smudged, tawny fur camouflaged in autumn's rich colours.

We'll never find her. We'll never get her home. And the farmers will come after her with their guns.

It was a horrible thought. She'd only known Cora for a day, and was still a bit nervous in her presence, but she couldn't bear the thought of the beautiful creature being harmed.

Luka was walking back to the quad bike, swinging himself on to the seat. Before he started the engine, he spoke again, his voice defensive.

"I'm not some kind of gun-freak. Grandpa and me only shoot animals for food. I get why you two want to protect the lynx, I really do. But we need to take care of the flock. Those sheep are our livelihood. We can't let this happen to them. They can't get away with this."

He turned the key, started the bike, shouting over the sound of the engine. "Morag Campbell and Ross Bauld are the ones to blame, not us! They're the ones who've put wild animals where they don't belong."

As the quad bike rumbled off, Esme and Callum watched it go, while Shug strained at his lead, keen to play chases, his fear of the gunshot forgotten.

"I guess he's right," sighed Esme. "Wolves and lynx don't belong in the Highlands. This isn't their natural home."

For a long moment Callum didn't reply, just focused on releasing Shug, who was so delighted to be free, he hared off towards the burn and splashed through the shallow water, snapping at insects and wallowing in the mud like a hippo. When the boy finally spoke, his voice was so loud that Esme jumped.

"You're wrong, actually."

"No, I'm not, *actually*. I'm a hundred percent right. Wolves and lynx live in the forests of Eastern Europe and North America. *Everyone* knows that."

"Yeah, but they used to live here too, long ago. When Sadie first told me about Cora, I googled lots of information. Scotland *is* the natural home of both lynx and wolves. In medieval times, lynx were hunted to extinction for their pelts and because farmers were concerned for their livestock. The last wolf was killed here in the seventeenth century. These animals have got as much right to live here as you and me and Luka Rydeski. This is their home."

Esme screwed up her face, exasperated with him for not understanding the obvious.

"Maybe it was okay to have wild animals roaming around in the olden days, when there were fewer people and houses, and zero cars, but Scotland's changed too much. It's too dangerous to have wild animals roaming free. Someone could get killed. And I mean, even if nobody gets killed, what's the actual point of having these animals around?"

Callum sighed, as if Esme had just said something incredibly stupid.

"The point is, that without a top predator, the whole eco-system stops working properly. There are too many deer and they're causing terrible damage. Forests are being overgrazed and stripped of vegetation. We need our big predators back."

She was about to snap that big predators weren't needed because deer culls were a thing, but Callum was still ranting.

"Campbell and Bauld have the right idea, though personally I don't think fenced enclosures, however big, are the answer. Too much like giant zoos. Wolves and lynx need to be free, so we need to find the best wild places for them, and maybe Rothiecraig isn't the right place. It doesn't mean there's no point in rewilding Scotland."

Esme shook her head, unimpressed, grabbed the water container and stood up, keen to have the last word on the matter.

"Doubt the farmers or the skiers or the Munro climbers will agree with you there. The last thing they want is to bump into a pack of wolves or a herd of lynx when they're out on the hills. It sounds crazy to me."

Callum's laugh was mocking. "A *herd* of lynx? *Really*?"

While Esme collected water, dowsed their campfire and ensured the ash and embers were cool, with no chance of reigniting, Callum washed the cups in the stream and put the empty Pot Noodle tubs in their rubbish bag. At least the rucksacks were getting lighter, she thought, as she dragged her rucksack onto her shoulders, if only because they'd eaten most of the food.

As they walked, the weather deteriorated. Rain clouds massed overhead, and it began to drizzle. Esme's feet dragged. Without Cora, it seemed pointless to continue the journey, but Callum's face was set and determined, and he marched on ahead. By the time they reached Ailcroft, Esme's legs and shoulders were aching and she had a painful stitch in her side. Even Shug's spirits had lowered. As they approached the ruined farmhouse, his tail drooped between his back legs and he started to whine.

"It's a bit spooky here." Esme dumped her rucksack on the ground. Rain was falling, splattering against her cheeks, and she didn't think she'd ever felt so cold and damp. It was hard to believe anyone had lived here, so far from civilisation, but the ancient building told a different story with the remains of a stone fireplace and a broken, rusted plough. Shug seemed to sense the presence of ghosts and refused to go anywhere near the tumbled walls of the old farmhouse.

There was no chance of lighting the fire tonight, and so they pitched the tents near the crumbled wall of a barn and sat together in Callum's tent, eating cold spaghetti and the rest of the bread. Shug squirmed at Esme's side, begging for bread scraps and eating them in one gulp. Outside, torrential rain fell, and a fierce wind tugged at the fragile frame.

Callum swallowed a spoonful of spaghetti and pulled a face. "You weren't wrong about the rubbish quality of the food. I can't wait to go home and have a decent meal." He wiped his mouth on the back of his sleeve. "If Cora doesn't turn up, there's not much point in continuing, is there? I really hoped she'd reappear when she got hungry."

Esme chewed on her lip. She'd have liked to tell him he'd been brave, that he'd saved Cora's life when he'd shoved Luka. But sitting side by side together in the tiny tent felt awkward enough.

"If she doesn't come back in the morning, I guess we'll have to go home and tell Gran and Sadie we didn't make it."

"Yeah, I guess so." Callum sounded miserable, his voice drained of energy.

Standing up, Esme hovered, keen to say something, *anything*, that might cheer him up, but afraid he'd sneer.

So instead, she spoke to the dog.

"Come on Shug, it's time for bed. You can guard me against the ghosts of Ailcroft."

As she stepped out into the pouring rain, Esme wished she hadn't put that thought in her head. It was all too easy to imagine pale wraiths floating among the abandoned outbuildings. Getting rain-soaked was as close as she was going to get to a wash, and having a pee in the pitiful shelter of the ruined barn was a grim experience. Rain clouds blanketed the sky, and though it was only seven o'clock, darkness was falling fast. It was a massive relief to get into her tent, switch on the torch and cuddle into her sleeping bag with Shug at her feet.

There's no such thing as ghosts. The people who lived here were ordinary farmers, a family with kids probably. Nothing evil about them. As long as this tent doesn't blow away, I'll be fine here until morning.

And then she heard a sound, distant but clear, that chilled her blood. Shug heard it too, and whined, wriggling to get as much of his body as possible underneath the sleeping bag.

"It's okay, boy. It's alright." She was trying to comfort herself as much as the dog. Because it wasn't alright. Somewhere, out there in the rainy darkness, a creature was howling.

The wind plucked at the fabric of the tent, and Esme shivered, her imagination in overdrive. Was it the tortured spirit of a murdered farmer… a blood hungry were-wolf?

She wasn't sure which option was worse.

But the noise stopped, suddenly, in mid-howl. She raised her head and listened, but apart from the thud of the rain and the whistle of the wind, there was silence in the camp. Callum was probably huddled in his tent, reading his book, and she wondered if he'd heard the howling too. But as the minutes passed, and Shug settled and began to snore, she wondered if her imagination had got the better of her. Perhaps it had been gusts of wind, wailing in the trees. Eventually, exhaustion won, and she pulled the sleeping bag up over her head and fell asleep.

8

ESME

A loud pattering against the tent's thin fabric woke Esme. It was morning and it was still raining, heavily. Shug had been fast asleep, curled close, his furry head on her feet, but as soon as she moved, the dog woke, and wormed his way along the side of the tent until he was close enough to lick her face.

"Get off, you daft dog." She pushed him away and wriggled further down into her sleeping bag. "You've got stinky breath!"

Usually, Shug would be whining to get outside first thing in the morning, desperate for a pee, but he snuggled up beside her, clearly preferring to stay in the warmth of the tent to being outside on this dreich morning. Esme stroked the dog's matted fur, her fingers snagging in the tangles, and listened to the drumming of the rain.

I'm staying right here. No way I am leaving the tent until that stops. Callum can go on his own, if he wants.

But she knew she wouldn't stay behind if Callum announced it was time to pack up. There was safety in numbers, even if their numbers were small. Last night's strange howl seemed dreamlike now, as imagined as the ghosts in the farmyard, but Ailcroft was too creepy, too isolated. She'd be glad to leave this place, even if it was hard to contemplate getting out of the tent.

For another hour she lay, snuggled in her sleeping bag, while Shug snored, rain fell and her thoughts whirled.

This journey's even worse than I thought it would be. We've lost Cora, the weather's awful, Callum despises me, and I hate him…

But was it true? Had she ever hated him, or had she just been mimicking Isobel? Picking her feelings apart was as tricky as untangling the pile of ropes in the P.E. cupboard. The uncomfortable truth was there was something likeable about Callum, particularly out here in the wilds, where he didn't have to be constantly on guard, as he did at school. He was knowledgeable and practical, and he seemed to genuinely care about what happened to Cora. He was kind to daft Shug.

But there's no hope of us two ever being friends. Not after everything that's happened at school. Not after all the mean things I've said and done.

A tear trickled down her cheek and she let it fall. Shug seemed to sense her unhappiness, nuzzled closer, and whined.

"It's okay. We'd better get up now, eh? Don't want you peeing in the tent."

It had gone quiet. The rain had stopped. When she unzipped the tent, a chilly breeze lifted the flap and shook it.

Early morning mist, filmy as a gauze shawl, draped the mountains and hung over the farm buildings. Weak sunlight slanted through violet-tinged clouds, leaving most of the glen in gloom. But where the sun shone, the colours gleamed: russet and ochre and gold. There was no sign of Callum, but his backpack was there, propped against the barn wall, so at least she knew she hadn't been left behind.

Esme took Shug for a short walk and then fed him some of the dried dog food. There were only a couple of portions left, and Shug gulped it down as if he was starving. Her own stomach was rumbling; she would have loved a hot drink. She pictured herself at Gran's, warming her feet by the stove, drinking tea from a heavy mug, waiting for the boiled eggs to be ready and for the toast to pop up and be cut into *soldiers*, as Gran called them.

Tomorrow. I'll be home on Monday evening. But what will Gran say when I tell her we've lost Cora? She's going to be so upset.

As Esme and Shug clambered over another hillock, she saw Callum, hood pulled up, back turned. He turned and put his fingers to his lips.

"Keep hold of Shug."

With a firm grip on the dog's collar, Esme walked over. When she reached Callum's side, she stopped dead and didn't say a word. Something incredible was happening, right in front of their eyes.

Cora was only a few metres away, but the lynx's tawny fur rendered her almost invisible in the dead foliage. Her body was so low, her furry stomach brushed the ground—she was stalking prey. Tense as a coiled spring, she crept forward, her amber eyes fixed on her victim: a plump grouse, pecking at dirt, oblivious to the danger. Esme's first instinct was to shout, to warn the poor bird, but she forced herself to stay quiet. Shug tried to pull free but he didn't bark, as if he too was curious to see what would happen next.

Mouth clamped shut, holding her breath, Esme watched as Cora inched ever closer to the bird. And then, without a sound, the lynx sprang. It seemed to happen in slow motion: the panicking bird fluttering upwards, just as Cora leapt, sailing, paws extended, a cat-superhero in flight. A short, terrified squawk tore the quiet as the lynx brought the grouse down. Cora landed in the tangle of bracken, a triumphant expression in her eyes, a smear of blood in her fluffy white beard, the dead bird dangling from her jaws.

Esme looked at Callum, just as he glanced at her.

"She did it." His voice was hoarse. "She can feed herself in the wild. She can live independently."

Esme beamed. Her feet felt light and springy, as if heavy weights had been removed.

"Don't you feel dead proud?"

He nodded, a half-smile on his face. "Yeah, it's like we taught her to do this, even though I know she's just following her instincts."

A downy feather floated past, and Esme was sure she could hear teeth crunching on bone.

"I don't really want to watch her eating the poor bird. Let's leave her to it. Do you want a cereal bar? It's too damp to build a fire."

"Aye, but I've got a wee gas stove in my pack." Callum's grin was so wide, his crooked front teeth were all visible.

"You've got a WHAT?" spluttered Esme. "I ate mingin cold spaghetti last night and you have a stove we could have used?"

Callum laughed. "Cold spaghetti's all part of the adventure! I was saving the stove for a weather emergency but last night's storm was a bit too extreme. We can heat up some beans and open the sachets of hot chocolate to celebrate Cora's success."

They didn't talk much on the long walk out of the glen but the atmosphere felt more cheerful. The sweet, scalding hot chocolate warmed Esme's insides, and Cora's triumph made her glow with happiness. It was Sunday; by tomorrow evening they'd have completed their journey and would be heading home. Her gran would be delighted with her. Everything was going to be fine.

When they stopped for lunch, Callum pointed out a herd of red deer on the hillside. Both of them stood, open mouthed in awe, when a golden eagle soared overhead.

He was right. As long as we stick to discussing Cora and the local wildlife, we'll get on fine. But what will happen when we go back to school? Do we go back to being enemies, even though Isobel and me are no longer friends?

Their day was going so well, but when they reached Crossford, where they'd hoped to camp, it seemed their journey had reached its end. Last night's rain had turned the shallow ford into a raging torrent. A river of brown, frothing water barred their way.

"That's not good." Esme was confident in water, but she wasn't reckless and knew the dangers of powerful currents only too well. "We can't cross here. We'll need to walk further downstream."

Callum didn't argue. It was all too clear the ford was impassable. The ground was boggy and the way hard going, but eventually they reached a narrower, less fast-flowing stretch of water. Esme searched until she found a long branch that had been tossed downstream and ended up wedged between two rocks. She tugged the branch free and unfastened her boots. "I'm going to check the depth. Wait here. Hold on to Shug."

She rolled up her trousers and stepped into the icy

water, so cold it felt like her feet were burning. Cautiously, she began to walk across the stream, using the stick to test the water's depth before every step, taking care not to slip on slimy stones or squelch in too-deep mud. The river's current surged round her calves and dragged at her feet, trying to pull her over. But the water wasn't deep. It was easy enough to stay upright, although mid-stream, she had to roll her trousers right up, so they dug into the skin on her thighs. When she reached the other side safely, she waved.

"It's fine. Shallow all the way."

As soon as she called, Callum let go of Shug's collar. The dog leapt in the water and doggy-paddled across the stream. While Esme dried her feet, she watched him, a smile on her lips. Shug was enjoying himself, eager to reach her. It was only when the dog got out the water and shook himself hard, spraying icy water over her already frozen legs, that Esme thought of Cora.

Cats hate getting wet.

"Callum, you'll need to bribe Cora with some meat!"

He'd heard her, she could tell, because he pulled the plastic box from his backpack, took out a strip of meat and waved it towards Cora, only just within view. Since her kill this morning, the lynx had begun to keep her distance, as if her newfound hunting skills were pulling her back to the wild.

Cora sniffed the air and approached Callum. His

boots were already off, jeans rolled up and backpack hitched high. As the lynx got nearer, Callum stepped into the water, and began to cross, walking backwards, waving the strip of dried meat in the air. But Cora didn't follow. She watched, and her nose was high, sniffing the air, but she didn't move.

Callum reached the other side and dropped his backpack on higher ground.

"We can set up camp here. Hopefully, Cora will come too, though we can't make her. Now that she can feed herself, we've got a problem. If she wants to, Cora can abandon us and go and live wild, alone on the moorland. She has no idea that she risks being shot by angry sheep farmers. She doesn't know to distrust humans."

Even when they'd put up the tents, and lit a campfire, Cora was still at the other side of the river, watching them, but refusing to step into the freezing water. Shug tried really hard to persuade her. He swam back across and tried to round her up, barking and circling, while the lynx gazed at him, expressionless. Esme got worried that Cora was hungry enough to pounce and called the dog back; he returned immediately, obedient for once, probably relieved that his lynx-dog services were no longer required.

Esme had been hoping the lynx would stick around until they reached the relative safety of Rothiecraig. But would the lynx cross the stream or decide the time had come for her to go her own way?

Maybe this is the end. If Cora leaves, there's no point carrying on with our journey. We'll need to pack up and go home.

To Esme's surprise, the thought made her sad. She wanted to finish what they'd started and make her grandmother proud. And she wanted Cora to be safe. Out here, she wasn't safe at all.

Callum, who'd been poking at the fire with a stick, trying to encourage damp wood to burn, leapt to his feet. "Can you keep an eye on the fire? I'm going to have another try, see if there's any way of getting her to come over."

Pulling off his boots and taking off his jacket and jumper, he went back into the water, waving the dried meat, and calling Cora.

The lynx's ears twitched, and she took a step forward. Her hunger was winning over her dislike of getting her fur wet. Coming to the water's edge, she placed a furry paw in the stream, seeming untroubled by the cold. Slowly, cautiously, she padded into the stream. When the water got deeper, she swam, furry head raised, a pained expression on her face.

She was almost across when a roaring sound came from upstream, and a churning wave of muddy water knocked Callum off his feet. Gasping and choking, he came up for air. Heart racing, Esme jumped up, grabbed the branch and held it out, stretching as far as she could reach. Shug stood at the water's edge, barking with excitement, convinced this was a fun new game.

"Grab the end!" Esme yelled, but Callum had no chance. He was mid-stream now, well out of reach, being tossed around by the force of the current, being dragged further downstream.

And he didn't seem to have a clue how to swim.

Even Shug seemed to sense this wasn't right. His bark had become high-pitched, panicky, and he ran over to Esme, leaping up at her, his claws scratching her legs.

Esme's heart crashed against her ribs. She was a member of the swimming team and had done a basic life-saving course, but in a heated pool, with a rubber brick, not with a real human caught in a raging torrent. But she couldn't leave Callum to drown, and there was nobody else around to help them, so she ran along the bank, trying to avoid tripping over Shug, who was bounding along beside her, barking frantically, being his completely useless self. When she was ahead of Callum, she stopped and pulled off her boots and outer clothes.

"Stay here, Shug. Do you hear me? Stay!"

Taking a deep breath, Esme leapt into the water, and gasped at the stinging cold. For a moment, the swirling currents dragged her under, and she felt panic clutch at her throat. But the water wasn't deep. Her feet touched rock, and she kicked out, propelling herself forwards and upwards through the current towards the boy's tumbling, flailing body.

Front crawl was Esme's best stroke, and she reached Callum in seconds. When she grabbed him, he didn't struggle, and lay so limp as she swam one-handed to shore that she was afraid he'd drowned. But as soon as she reached the side, he struggled to his feet, and stood, bent over, gasping and retching, while Shug licked at his face, delighted the humans had seen sense and returned to dry land.

"Where's Cora? Is she alright?"

Esme pointed towards a clump of Scots pines. She'd seen the lynx, fur dripping and bedraggled, clambering out of the water as she'd jumped into save Callum, but the sight had barely registered.

"She's safe, and I saw her heading in there. But we need to get dry. We're no use to Cora if we've got hypothermia."

She gave him a shove towards his tent and went into her own to change into dry clothes. When she came back out, she hung her wet things on a tree branch, next to Callum's, and hoped the sun would come out in the morning. Luckily the fire had managed to stay alight, and Cora, attracted by its warmth, had slunk back into camp and was sprawled in front of it. Shug was curled near her, steam rising from his damp coat. Esme felt a grin of satisfaction spread across her face.

Everyone's here. We're all okay.

She sat down between the two animals. "Well done, Shug," she whispered. "Good lass, Cora."

Shug's tail thudded against the ground. He licked Esme's hand and wriggled closer, so his head lay heavy across her legs. Cora didn't react with the same enthusiasm, but she didn't seem to mind Esme's presence. Her beautiful face, mouth curved in a half-smile, was relaxed, and her golden eyes half closed. But then she yawned, showing sharp canines, flattened like knife blades, and Esme edged a little further away.

Callum's right. It's so tempting to treat Cora as an overgrown pet, but she's a wild animal. And if she's going to survive in the world she needs to learn to avoid humans. It isn't fair to encourage her to trust us.

The tomato soup Callum was heating in the pan smelled delicious. However, it was hot enough to melt glass, and the first gulp burnt her tongue. Esme laid the cup on the grass, waiting for it to cool, and gazed into the flickering flames, enjoying their warmth.

"You never said you couldn't swim."

Callum shrugged. "I never stayed long enough in a foster placement to finish a block of lessons, and some of my foster parents didn't bother at all."

Every time he was moved, he had to start again with a different family, and at a new school. It must have been so hard. It must have been awful.

But she hesitated, guilt curdling in her stomach, not knowing what to say. His childhood *did* sound awful, but she and Callum weren't friends, and had only agreed to a temporary halt to hostilities. She guessed he wouldn't want her sympathy. Not now, when she'd spent so long being horrible to him.

Focusing on tearing off a chunk of stale bread, Esme gave a piece to Shug and dipped the rest in the soup. By the time she'd finished eating, the silence had gone on for so long, it had become a glass wall, and she felt she needed to break it.

"My dad and mum split up years ago. He works on the oil-rigs and stays in a flat in Peterhead." When Esme thought of her lovely dad—his crinkly smile and bear hugs, the smell of his spicy aftershave, the love in his warm, deep voice—her heart melted like chocolate. "He comes to see me every few weeks, when he can get time off work."

And when he can face dragging himself away from his new life with Elspeth and Flora and Madeline. He always comes for a visit, never asks me to stay. Cos he bought a two-bedroom flat and the twins already share. There's no room for me. And if Elspeth's not well, or he has to take the girls to a party, he cancels on me. His new family come first. Every time.

But Esme wasn't prepared to tell anyone that. She could hardly bear to admit it to herself. Callum stayed silent, but she managed to pluck up the courage to ask the question she'd been longing to ask.

"Do you still see your birth family at all?"

His dark eyes glistened in the firelight, and he spoke so quietly she had to strain to hear him.

"I've never met my dad. Mum's a drug addict. She… she couldn't cope with me and my wee brother. The neighbours got worried about the constant shouting and crying and called social services. They tried to keep us together as a family, but when she'd left us on our own without food once too often, Robbie and me got taken away and put in care."

Callum reached for his pile of firewood and broke a branch over his knee. Even though she was expecting it, the loud crack made Esme jump. When he threw the wood in the fire, sparks leapt and fizzled on the grass. Shug started barking, and disturbed by the noise, Cora woke and moved further away from the fire. As if he sensed the boy's distress, Shug moved from Esme's side, and laid his head on Callum's knee.

"The plan was to have us both adopted as a 'sibling group'." Bitterness seethed in Callum's voice. "But it didn't happen like that. My brother Robbie was a cute two-year-old, and a couple wanted to adopt him, but they didn't want me. So, I lost him too."

Tears stung Esme's eyelids, and she brushed them away with her sleeve.

"I'm so sorry, Callum." And she was. She was sorry for everything. But she couldn't go back, couldn't change what she'd done. It was far too late.

9

CALLUM

Anxiety fluttered in Callum's stomach as he checked the map. After such a late start, were they still on target to reach Rothiecraig estate by the afternoon? If they arrived after dark, it was going to be impossible to ensure Cora was safe. And he and Esme still had to persuade Cora to stay with them for one more day. They had miles to go and lots of obstacles to face before he could go home. And he was desperate to go home, back to the warmth of the croft, and Sadie's gruff company. He missed her, and he knew she'd be missing him, and he hadn't felt like that since being separated from Robbie.

He walked on, putting Crossford behind him, striding ahead of Esme. It was a beautiful morning, and the sun felt warm on his back. Sunlight was glittering on the lochan. The landscape's autumn colours glowed, jewel-bright. A few more miles, and they'd be there. If the weather held, they'd make it easily. Last night, they'd agreed to wait until noon to decamp, to give their clothes and the tents time to dry, and luckily they'd woken to bright morning sunlight, glinting on a river that was no longer a churning torrent of mud. After all of yesterday's drama, it had been good to have a breathing space, time to sit and read beside the river, though he'd stayed quiet, preferring not to get pulled into conversation with Esme. He was still annoyed with himself for telling her so much about his past last night.

What an eejit… I should have kept my big mouth shut. What was I thinking? She's bound to tell Isobel about my mum, and about Robbie, and then the whole class will know. They'll never let it drop. Your mum's a druggie… nobody wanted you…

It was stuff he hadn't even talked to Sadie about, though he knew she'd have read it in his copious notes. So why on earth had he told Esme McKinnon?

He kicked a pebble into the lochan and heard a loud splash as Shug jumped in after it, and doggy-paddled through the deep water, snapping at air.

"Here, boy! Come back!"

He heard Esme's boots, crunching on gravel, as she ran along the narrow beach that circled the lochan. Her voice sounded panicked, and no wonder, after what had happened yesterday.

"He's fine. Don't worry. Look, he's heading back to shore. Must be freezing in that water."

They both watched as Shug clambered out, and stood well back while he shook himself.

"You're very quiet." When Esme spoke, Callum felt his muscles tense, preparing for flight. "Are you feeling okay after your... um... swim yesterday?"

"Yeah, I'm fine. And it's great to feel warm sunshine, for a change." He hesitated, remembering that there was something he'd forgotten to do. "Thanks, by the way. You saved my life. I didn't know you were such a good swimmer."

"Yeah, I was in the local swim team, until Isobel told me I was starting to smell of chlorine."

"Wow. And do you always listen when Isobel talks mince?"

Her face flamed so red, it clashed with her hair. "I used to. Not anymore." She looked away from him, gazing at the water. Its bright, mirrored surface had been disturbed by a breeze; tiny waves rippled on the lochan's surface. "I won't say a word to anyone about the things you told me last night. I know you probably don't believe me, but it's the truth. I promise."

He nodded, the tension seeping from him like air from a burst tyre. "Thank you."

And then, almost invisible among the trees, he caught a glimpse of a short, black-tipped tail, a flash of spotted fur. "Look, Cora's coming. See her, walking down to the lochan? She must be thirsty."

When Esme spotted the lynx, she smiled, joy shining in her eyes. The sun had sprinkled even more freckles on

Esme's nose and her hair stood in tufts, like an elf's. Her smile was wide and genuine. She looked so friendly that it was hard to imagine she was the same girl he loathed in school, the one with the smirk and the mocking laugh.

Does she mean what she says, though? Will she keep quiet about the things I told her? And has she really had enough of being in Isobel's gang? Or will everything go back to 'normal' when we're back at school on Wednesday?

They walked together, keeping almost in step, leaving the lochan behind, approaching the hilly, wooded land surrounding Rothiecraig. Both of them kept looking around, to check on Cora's whereabouts. Even Shug seemed to sense that the lynx was important, and kept doubling back, giving encouraging barks, though Callum suspected the barks were counter-productive.

Cora was following them, at a distance, keeping them in sight, torn between her instinct to hide and her desire to seek out human company.

"Maybe we will need to scare her tonight. I mean, we need to make sure she'll avoid humans for the rest of her life."

Esme pulled a face. "I know it's the right thing for her, but it's a horrible thought."

But tonight's worry faded into the background. Something was wrong, right now. Three horribly familiar things lay on the ground ahead. Even Shug seemed anxious, running towards one, sniffing at it and then racing to another, whining and barking.

"Shug, leave those sheep alone!" called Esme. "Don't disturb them when they're sleeping."

"The sheep won't mind." Callum couldn't be a hundred percent certain from this distance, but he was sure enough. "They're dead."

And they hadn't just fallen down dead. They'd been savaged. As he came closer, he could see that their fleeces were grimy and bloodstained. And each had gaping wounds, torn throats.

"Shug! Come here!" His voice was sharper than he'd intended, so loud that the pair of hoodie crows, perched in the berry-laden rowan tree nearby, flapped their wings and flew off. Shug for once, did as he was told, and Esme slipped on his lead, keeping him at a distance.

As Callum drew nearer, he pulled his scarf over his nose. The smell of rotting flesh was vile. Flies buzzed around the corpses and when Callum reached them, the flies rose in a cloud. He shuddered at the sight of the animals' empty eye sockets and thought of the two hoodie crows.

Esme stood a short distance away, a hand over her mouth. "They've been dead for a while, haven't they?" She leant forward, eyes closed, and Callum wondered if she was going to be sick. "I can smell them from here."

Callum nodded. "Yes, they've been dead a few days, I reckon. I wonder what's happened."

Esme's head jerked up. She fixed him with an accusing stare.

"You know very well what's happened, Callum Docherty! Don't pretend you haven't heard the howling in the night." She looked around, as if expecting to see a pack of wolves slinking towards them. "The wolves have escaped and they're out there somewhere, prowling about on the moor, attacking sheep, aren't they?"

Callum didn't answer. He stared at the dead animals, wondering, trying to remember all the facts he'd googled about wolves.

Wolves don't kill for sport. They kill to eat. However, rarely, they'll kill more than they can eat at the one time, especially when food is scarce in late winter, and they'll return to the food caches again and again. But it isn't winter. It's September. Food shouldn't be scarce.

"It was the wolves, wasn't it?" persisted Esme. She seemed more angry than scared, as if he'd been keeping the wolves a secret from her. And maybe he had, but she'd just admitted she'd heard them too, and she'd said nothing. Maybe, she felt the same as he did. Once daylight arrived, the howling in the night seemed unreal, belonging to a bad dream of werewolves and vampires.

"It might have been dogs. Sadie always says sheep have no common sense. They don't behave in the same way as other prey, like rabbits and deer. Sheep don't run away, they run in circles. Sadie says that's why dogs need to be kept on leads around sheep, because when all that panicky circling starts, dogs can get over-excited into making multiple kills. Maybe that what's happened here?"

"Yeah, and wolves are wild dogs, aren't they?"

He nodded. While it was still possible those sheep had been killed by a domestic dog, the evidence before them seemed impossible to ignore.

Apart from Shug, there's been no sign of dogs, either on the moor, or in the glen, and there's no way it was Shug, or Cora. These sheep have been dead for days. And... we both heard those eerie howls in the night. But the sheep must have wandered miles from the rest of the flock in the glen. Something very strange is going on.

Hitching up his rucksack, he started to move away from the smelly carcasses. "Luka Rydeski is going to freak when he finds these bodies. We had better get out of here, in case he blames Cora. Can you see her?"

Esme shook her head. "She's vanished again. But you're right. We need to get away from here. Let's go."

When they were downwind of the smelly sheep carcasses, Callum stopped, took one of the few remaining pieces of dried meat from the box and waved it around, hoping Cora would follow the scent. Beside him, Esme turned in a slow circle, one hand shading her face, her eyes clouded with worry.

"Maybe we shouldn't leave without Cora. After all,

she's hungry and she might try and eat one of those sheep. Rotting meat will make her ill, surely."

"We need to keep going."

He hadn't meant to sound so sharp, but it was true. Although it was worrying that Cora was no longer in sight, they couldn't hang around any longer, or it might be dark before they reached Rothiecraig. His eyes darted, hoping to catch a glimpse of Cora, but she was nowhere to be seen. He wished she'd stay close, the way the dog did, but why should she? She was a wild animal, not a docile, devoted pet like Shug, who was ambling along, taking his own circuitous route, involving a quick sniff round the base of every tree, and a half-hearted bite at every midge. Every couple of minutes he'd head back to check that his humans hadn't got lost.

Callum and Esme walked on and on in silence. An army of worries was massing in his head, all fighting for attention, and he wondered if Esme felt the same.

Even if Cora turns up, even if we manage to get her back to Rothiecraig, even if she's accepted by the other lynx, and according to my research that's pretty unlikely, she isn't going to be safe, with a shower of angry farmers after her. It isn't fair. She isn't involved in killing those sheep. It's the wolves… it has to be the wolves.

It wasn't a happy thought. He'd have loved to see wolves living in the wild, but not if it meant that he and Sadie would have to arm themselves and spend their nights guarding their own flock against attack. Sadie would have a fit if she lost any of her precious Blackface ewes, or Hector the ram, or her small flock of rare Soay sheep, to a pack of wolves.

When Callum and Esme stopped for lunch, at the foot of yet another hill, they didn't talk much. Esme stuck fresh plasters on her blistered heels, while he focused on lighting the fire and heating up their last can of soup. It was chicken and rice, and with half a packet of dry crackers, quite filling, but he found himself daydreaming of eating a late supper at home tonight: hot wholemeal toast, perhaps, dripping with honey and melted butter, or a scone with rich clotted cream and homemade raspberry jam.

He slurped the remains of his soup and stood up. "We'd better get a move on."

As Esme pulled on her backpack, she scanned the hillside, clearly searching for Cora. Her eyes were sad, her shoulders slumped with disappointment, but she said nothing, and he too kept his feelings to himself.

I'm looking forward to getting home. But I don't want to have to tell Sadie I've failed. And if being totally honest, I think it's over.

10

ESME

My foot hurts. I want to go home. I've had enough. We could be attacked by wolves at any moment. And what if we've lost Cora and this has all been a gigantic waste of time?

Esme's foot had started to hurt during the morning, but she'd tried to ignore it, until they stopped for lunch, when she tried to sort herself out, with new plasters and double socks. As she stuck on the plasters, it dawned on her that she hadn't worried about her appearance for ages. Out here, out of Isobel's reach, it didn't matter, and her short hair cut was perfect for the moors. Drying long hair, and keeping it out of the way, would have been a real nuisance.

During the afternoon, despite her efforts, the blisters on her heels nipped so badly the pain brought tears to her eyes. But there was no point talking to Callum. Since they'd come across those sheep carcasses, a black cloud seemed to have sunk over him, and he was quieter and more sullen than ever.

The pain from the blister on her left heel was terrible,

so she flung herself down on a rock, pulled off her boot and rummaged again for the box of plasters. Callum strode on, but Shug stayed with her, sniffing at her discarded sock and wagging his tail, as if the smell of her stinky feet pleased him hugely. The dog's presence was a comfort, until he grabbed the sock and she had to engage in a tug of war to retrieve it.

"Give that back, Shug! Stop being a pest!" The material had caught on the dog's sharp teeth, and when she pulled, the sock ripped. "Stupid dog. Look what you've done to my sock!"

Catching her sharp tone, Shug dropped the sock at Esme's feet, and gazed at her, reproach in his eyes. Guilt tightened in her stomach.

Poor Shug. He has been dragged away from home and has been a wee star the whole way, and now I'm being mean to him.

"Sorry, I didn't mean to snap. Look, my sock's fine. Hardly holey at all."

When she had tugged on the torn sock and added her last pair of dry socks on top, Esme looked across to the hills.

"Look, Callum's way ahead. We're getting left behind, and neither of us knows the way."

Shug lay his head on her knee and looked up at her with big, sad eyes. Esme ruffled his ears.

"Yeah, me too. We both wish we were in Gran's house

right now, don't we, boy? Cup of tea, warm fire, telly. Bone for you, homemade shortbread for me."

Shug wagged his tail, delighted by the prospect of a bone, or more likely, of shortbread.

Esme looked behind her, at the mountains, burnished gold in the afternoon sun, shielding Glen Craig from view. They'd crossed a rugged moor, travelled through a beautiful glen, stayed the night at a spooky, haunted farmhouse, crossed a swollen river. She'd rescued Callum from drowning. He'd saved Cora from being shot. They had come a long way, and she'd felt she and Callum were developing a better understanding. She'd even begun to like him. But now they seemed to be going backwards, and if Cora *had* decided to stay in the wild, their journey had been for nothing.

She sighed, got to her feet and hobbled after the figure in the distance. Shug bounded after her, panting with the effort.

Callum had stopped on the brow of a hill and was waiting for her. "We're here. Rothiecraig Estate. Look, the castle is just visible through the trees."

Esme searched Callum's face for clues and found it impossible to tell how he was feeling about the fact they'd reached their destination, but had lost their reason for setting out in the first place. She tried to look where he was pointing, but the low, afternoon sun was shining in her eyes. Squinting, she saw the top of a rectangular, grey-stone building. A tattered Saltire flew from the crumbling turret. The castle's windows were slits in the stonework, and reminded Esme of empty eye sockets. Spooked, she shivered. "Does Lady Campbell live in there? Are you sure she isn't a vampire?"

"Well, I guess she might be, but I'm pretty sure she doesn't live in the castle, since it doesn't have a roof. There's a big, posh mansion on the estate, according to Sadie."

"So, what's the plan? How do we access the estate?"

"We're already on it. This is Rothiecraig land. The estate is huge, masses of hectares. All we need to do, is get through the main gates, past the big house and find the sections that are surrounded by high fences, because that's the protected areas for the wolf and the lynx."

Except there isn't any point doing any of that, if Cora isn't here.

Another thought, which had been niggling at her since the start of the journey, surfaced. "Let's imagine that Cora does turn up. What's the plan? How will we get her back with her family? If the rest of the lynx are behind fences, I mean? Do we break in? Steal the key to the door? Or what?"

Callum didn't answer, just stood there, scratching at the dry skin on his bottom lip, and it dawned on Esme that he didn't have a plan for that part of their mission. The crucial part.

"Are you telling me you don't know?"

No wonder he'd been so withdrawn on this final section.

"Didn't you and Sadie talk about it, when you were planning together?"

"Well, we did. We talked about it, but we couldn't figure out how it could be done. Sadie just said an idea would come to us, she was sure of it."

"Did she now?" Esme couldn't keep the sarcastic note from her voice and saw Callum wince.

He increased his pace and despite her sore heel, she half-jogged to keep up.

It felt strange to finally reach a tarmacked road, after days of walking on moorland paths.

"Civilisation at last, Shug," she said, and then grabbed the dog's collar to stop him running in front of a logging lorry thundering past. "Careful, silly."

The main gates were wide, unlocked, as it was only three o'clock and the castle and its grounds were still open to the public. A large sign informed them that dogs must be kept on the lead, and as Esme clipped on Shug's, a car rumbled past, exiting the main estate.

"Did you see that?" Callum sounded incredulous. "The two kids in that car were holding fluffy toy wolves. There must be a souvenir shop here. I guess keeping wild animals pays."

As they approached the squat little gatehouse at the side of the drive, Callum gestured at the two vehicles parked in front of the building.

"Luka's quad bike is in the back of that truck! It must be the Rydeski's. We'd better hide before they see us."

At the sound of raised, angry voices, Shug slunk back, twisting his body round Esme's legs.

"It's okay, Shug," she whispered, crouching behind the cottage's gable wall beside Callum, so they could spy without being seen. "Keep quiet, there's a good boy."

A bearded man, who Esme recognised as Jan Rydeski, was standing with Luka beside their battered pick-up. He was shouting and waving his fist at a stocky, bald-headed man in a camouflage jacket, jeans and wellies.

"Four sheep I've lost recently, Bauld!" he yelled. "Those flaming wild beasts are massacring my flock. Instead of taking my ewes to market as we'd planned, I've got three savaged corpses in the back of my truck."

"Must be the sheep we came across," whispered Callum. "But if so, they were killed a long way from home."

Bauld held up his hands, as if in surrender.

"But, Jan, it can't have been the wolves. It must've been a stray dug. The Rothiecraig wolf pack's locked up securely, you can be sure of that."

"You can assure me all you like, but you'd be telling me lies! We've heard them howling, haven't we, Luka?"

Luka had been standing back slightly, one arm draped over the side of the other vehicle, a smart pick-up truck with bottle-green paintwork, the words *Rothiecraig Estate* written in gold along its side. At the mention of his name, he jumped as if he'd been shot.

"Um, yeah. I've heard wolves howling in the night, a couple of times this week."

Jan Rydeski moved closer to Bauld and loomed over him. "So, there are wolves on the loose. Four of our sheep have been savaged, throats torn open. It's wolves all right! I'm heading up to the house to speak to Morag Campbell right now!"

Ross Bauld's voice was smooth as butter, calm and reasonable. "There's no point doing that, Jan. She has paying guests up at the big hoose, about ten of them. They're here for a shooting weekend. Shooting wi a camera, would you believe it? What's the point of that? Anyway, she'll be raging if you turn up unannounced. I'm estate manager, so it's me you need to speak to first."

Jan Rydeski was red-faced with anger. Spit flew from his mouth as he yelled.

"This is the second time, you eejit! I was here yesterday about the first ewe and you told me it must have been a rambler's dog that killed her. Well, here I am again, and this time, I'm not leaving until you admit those wolves were responsible!"

Bauld gave a heavy sigh and scratched at his thinning hair. "I'll tell you what I'll do. You come into the cottage and we'll write up a report to sign, and I'll give it to Lady Campbell tonight. You'll be compensated if it turns out to be necessary. She'll take this issue seriously, you know.

Between you, me and the gatepost, she has a few doubts about the project. It's me who's been the main supporter of the idea from the start. But, if what you're saying's true…"

Jan Rydeski started to splutter again, and Bauld put an arm on the man's arm and led him towards the gatehouse. Luka followed, feet trailing, shoulders hunched.

"Luka doesn't look happy." In fact, the boy looked really troubled, and the expression on his face was making Esme's thoughts spin like clothes in a dryer. There was something about the way he had hung back, not engaging in the argument, that was making her suspicious.

Why's he not backing up his grandfather? Is he starting to have doubts that the wolves killed the sheep?

Callum tugged at her arm. "Luka Rydeski isn't our problem. Let's leave our backpacks here and go find the lynx and wolf enclosures. If Cora doesn't turn up, we'll just need to give up and leave. Sadie will be at the main gate at seven o'clock, and it's twenty past three now."

When she'd slipped off her backpack and hid it under a laurel bush, Esme straightened up and looked around, hoping for a glimpse of the lynx. But there was no sign of her.

Come on, Cora. Where are you? We're running out of time.

11

CALLUM

There were no signs directing tourists towards the lynx and wolf enclosures. Soft toy versions might be for sale in the shop, but it appeared Morag Campbell wasn't treating the Rothiecraig wolves and lynx as zoo exhibits.

All the signs pointed in the direction of the castle, the toilets and the café. A massive *Keep Out! Private!* sign kept visitors from wandering up the drive towards the big house. With no real idea about which direction to take, Callum headed into the forest. At first, it was a regular, regimented pinewood, but as they walked further, they reached a longer established woodland, a mixture of pine, oak and birch. When a startled roe deer leapt away from them, he watched it bound through the trees, and thought that this was an environment in which Cora might feel at home.

Esme caught up with Callum and hobbled along beside him. "I've been thinking," she said, excitement fizzing in her voice.

He was about to tell her that he was pleased to hear

it as he'd thought Isobel did all the thinking for her. But before the comment could shoot from his mouth he swallowed it down, annoyed with himself.

We're on a truce. This isn't school. Be nice.

"What about?" he managed instead, hoping that perhaps she had a plan, and had figured out how they could get into the lynx enclosure, because despite Sadie's confidence, no brilliant ideas were popping into his brain.

"I've been trying to work out what's going on, and I think I might have figured it out."

"And?"

"I reckon the farmers did it."

Callum laughed, and then felt guilty, because he could see from the look on her face that she was serious.

"Okay, so why do you think the farmers would do that to their own sheep?"

He heard her take a deep breath, and then her words rushed out in a torrent.

"Well, I figure there are two good reasons for the Rydeskis to lie about their sheep being killed by wolves. Number one, they're short of money. Luka said so, didn't he? So, perhaps they're trying to get compensation from Morag Campbell. I think it's all a scam."

Esme's eyes were fierce, daring him to argue. Even with her limping gait, she seemed more determined, more confident than she had at the beginning of their quest.

But it won't last, not once she's back at school, back to being Isobel's sidekick.

For a moment Callum didn't reply, mulling over what she'd said. Then, reluctantly, he shook his head. "I can see why you're saying that, but I honestly don't believe they'd do that. Those ewes were more valuable to them alive. They'd be hoping for lambs from them in February, and the next, and the next."

She nodded but didn't look completely convinced.

"Okay, fair enough, but you haven't heard my second reason. From what Luka said, he and his grandfather seem to hate the idea of re-introducing large predators to the Highlands, don't they?"

"You're dead right. And they're not the only ones. Most of the farmers around here, Sadie included, think it's a crazy idea."

Esme was bouncing with excitement, causing Shug to leap up and down too, as if they were both on trampolines.

"Exactly! So, I figure that the Rydeskis are afraid that if this project is a success and the idea of rewilding becomes more acceptable, wolves and lynx will eventually be allowed to roam free. So, they're trying to sabotage Lady Campbell's pilot project, by pretending her wolves have killed the sheep."

Esme was unable to disguise the note of triumph in her voice. She really thought she had it all figured out, and maybe she had.

Callum rubbed at his nose but kept walking. "There's only one small problem with your theory. Jan Rydeski mentioned that he and Luka had heard wolves howling. They weren't lying about that, were they? I heard them too—and so did you."

Her face clouded, then brightened. "Yes, but sound waves travel, don't they? So maybe we heard the Rothiecraig wolf pack howling from behind their fences."

"In a heavily forested place like this estate, that would be remarkable. I think the greatest distance a wolf howl has travelled is about ten miles, but that's on the tundra. In forested areas, howls travel between three and six miles. The Rydeski's farmhouse is a good fifteen miles away, at the far end of Glen Craig. Ailcroft is…"

His voice trailed away, as it dawned on him that Esme wasn't listening to a word. Balanced against a tree, she was standing on tiptoes, neck craned.

"Callum, look! I think it's Cora! Can you see her?"

He couldn't, not at first, but as his eyes adjusted to the dim light and the shadows cast by the Scots pines, he saw the long-legged lynx moving, quiet as a ghost, through the thick cover of the trees. Her head was high, and her tufted ears twitched as she took in the smells and sounds of Rothiecraig.

Does she sense she's nearly home? Can she smell her mother's scent?

"Quick, follow her." Callum left the path and hurried

through the woods, dragging Shug, hoping Esme would be able to keep up, desperate not to lose sight of Cora. But keeping tabs on the lynx was virtually impossible, as her spotted coat blended so perfectly with her surroundings. Every step he took, his jacket snagged on twigs, his boots caught on roots or sank in mud, but Cora padded serenely through the trees, completely at home in the forest.

If the herd of roe deer caught her scent, they'd be moving on, finding somewhere else to graze. And it would be a good thing for the forest, because if deer remained in one place, as they would if they had no predators, they were capable of causing terrible damage, stripping the bark from the older trees and fraying saplings with their antlers.

Within minutes, the lynx reached a high fence and stopped dead, her heavy head pressed hard against the mesh, inhaling scents Callum hoped felt familiar. Because this had to be it: the lynx enclosure. Cora had found her birthplace. She was almost home, but of course, she couldn't get in. Not here, anyway. The animal's head dropped low, sniffing the ground. Her huge, white paws padded, silent on soft leaf mould, along the outside of the fence, through a tangle of thorny brambles and creeping ivy.

Esme limped to a halt at Callum's side, grimacing, and guilt tugged at him. He'd constantly been pushing her to go faster, despite knowing her heels were blistered, and she was clearly in pain.

"We might have a long walk along the perimeter of this enclosure, to find the entrance. I can go on ahead if your foot's hurting? Do you want to rest for a while?"

She shook her head. "No, I do not. My blisters are gowping, but I'm not letting them stop me. This is too important, and I'm not giving up before Cora's home."

It startled him to realise he was glad. He'd thought Esme McKinnon's presence was going to make the journey unbearable, but it would have been a lonely one without her.

And I probably wouldn't have made it out of that river. She saved my life.

Esme put on the last of the plasters and retied her boots. "Where's Cora?"

"She's coming towards us. Over there, see? She's pacing this section of fence. I think she's trying to get in."

As they watched, Cora began to make a strange noise, one they'd never heard her make before, a weird cross between a yowl and a bark. Esme tugged at the ivy curling up the fence and peered through the mesh. Then she grabbed Callum's arm, making him jump.

"There's another lynx! A big, brown one. Hiding in the trees behind the fence! Do you think that's her mother?"

But if it was, the captive lynx wasn't happy to see her long-lost daughter. Growling, mouth curled in a snarl, eyes flashing an amber warning, the larger lynx launched its body against the fence, claws extended, jaws wide. Yelping with fear, Shug scurried backwards, his paws scrabbling on wet, slippery leaf mould, pulling on the lead so hard he almost dragged Callum off his feet. In contrast to Shug's fear, Cora didn't seem particularly bothered by the spitting fury of the other lynx. Even when the lynx attacked again, throwing itself so hard against the fence that the mesh twanged, Cora continued to pace the fence, making her odd, yowling bark.

After another, half-hearted attempt at reaching Cora, the bigger animal gave up the attack. They could hear menacing growls as the lynx paced for a while, mirroring Cora's movements. But then Callum looked through the gap in the ivy Esme had created, and caught a glimpse of a stubby, black-tipped tail, as the captive lynx headed back into the depths of the forested enclosure.

Callum's feelings of horror were mirrored in Esme's face.

"Do you think that was Cora's mum? Do you think she's forgotten her?"

"I don't know. I didn't get a clear enough view to tell whether that lynx was male or female. And I told you already, lynx are solitary animals, very territorial, and they only come together in the short mating season. Behaviour like that is totally natural for a lynx."

He rubbed at his face with his sleeve, trying and

failing to stop tears brimming in his eyes. It *was* natural behaviour, but not between a mother and her cub, surely. Unless Cora had been totally rejected and become an unloved outcast. It hurt his heart to hear her, still making those weird, plaintive cries and it was clearly hurting Esme too. Her voice sounded choked.

"Do you think we're doing the wrong thing, trying to put her back in there? She could be killed!"

His mouth opened and closed and opened again, and for a moment, no words emerged at all.

He sat down on the stump of a dead tree, ran a hand through his hair. It felt greasy, unwashed. He was in dire need of a shower.

"I reckon we've got to carry on. We can't take her back to your gran's house, can we? So, we need to find the entrance to the lynx enclosure and somehow, get her inside."

"And then, she's on her own?"

He gave a helpless shrug. "How can we protect her, Esme? Cora is a wild animal. At least we know she can catch her own food. It would have been lovely if she could have been reunited with her mother, but fairy tale happy endings don't exist. Cora will need to find her own territory, and perhaps she'll be fine on her own."

Esme nodded, but her face was drawn and sad. "She's so small, compared to the full-size lynx. She wouldn't stand a chance in a fight. But you're right. We don't have a lot of time left. We'd better look for the entrance."

Behind them, a male voice boomed. "I wouldn't recommend doing that. There are wild animals in there."

Startled, Esme and Callum spun round, to face the estate manager striding towards them. Ross Bauld wasn't a tall man, but he was well-muscled. Naturally, Shug was thrilled to see him, and clearing thinking this stranger would share his delight, jumped up, tail flailing, muddy paws scrabbling at the man's trouser legs, attempting slobbery kisses. Bauld pushed Shug down, too roughly, Callum thought, but didn't say, because he was anxious not to get on the man's wrong side.

"This area's out of bounds to tourists, kids—and for guid reason. Get yoursels back to the castle and the play park!" Bauld's tone was jovial, but there was no warmth in his eyes.

Before Callum could say anything, Esme spoke up. "We're just having a wee look, to see if we can spot any lynx. We'll only be five minutes. It's for a school project, you see."

Ross Bauld shook his head. "Sorry, but it's mair than my job's worth. Do as you're tellt, and run along and find your maw. It'll be closing time in twenty minutes, and you don't want to be trapped here after dark, wi they vicious big cats, just waitin to pounce on careless weans."

Smiling broadly, Bauld made a shooing gesture. Callum was about to argue, when out of the corner of his eye, he glimpsed a blackbird flutter upwards, chirping frantically. Cora had walked further round the perimeter than she'd done the first few times, but she was clearly heading back now.

Holding up his hands, as if in surrender, Callum smiled. "No worries. We're just leaving, aren't we, Esme?"

"But…" She stopped and he saw her eyes widen. She'd clearly spotted Cora's approach too. "Yes, we need to go. Could you show us the way back? We're a bit lost."

"'Fraid no. Some of us have work to do." Bauld grimaced and held up a toolbox.

As Callum and Esme walked away, Shug tugged at the lead, keen to say goodbye to this smiling stranger. Callum turned back, to pull the dog away, and saw Shug lick Bauld's hand. The man's mouth curled in a snarl. Before Callum could do anything to prevent it happening, Bauld kicked out. His boot thudded against Shug's ribs, so hard the dog squealed.

"Leave him alone!" Pulling the dog out of Bauld's reach, anger tightened Callum's chest.

Bauld pulled a face, pretending to be in pain. "That ruddy dug bit me."

He didn't. He wouldn't. You're a liar.

But Callum said nothing, because Cora had just emerged from the bramble bushes, and was standing directly behind them. His heart pounded, terrified that Bauld would spot her.

Turn round, lass. Go back. Keep out of sight.

As if she'd heard him, Cora lifted her head, and sniffed the air, then started walking back the way she'd come, body brushing against the fence, her stubby tail swinging like the pendulum on a clock. As the tail disappeared into the thick undergrowth, Callum breathed again.

"Get the bloody dug out of here!" Bauld's fake cheeriness had vanished, and with the smile gone from his face, he looked and sounded vicious. It occurred to Callum that Sadie had been brave to pick an argument with Ross Bauld.

As Callum dragged Shug away, Esme followed, limping.

They'd gone a short distance, when Callum looked back and saw that Bauld was walking along the enclosure's fence, swinging his toolbox, seeming untroubled by his 'injury'.

"He's not watching us. Get down!"

Ducking down behind a holly bush they crouched, holding tightly to Shug, who laid his head on Esme's knee and whimpered. Callum patted the injured dog and swore under his breath.

"What kind of creep would kick poor Shug?"

"He's an evil pig." Esme's voice shook with anger. "I bet he's up to no good. I bet he's…"

Callum put his finger to his lips. "Listen! Bauld said he had work to do here, didn't he? Maybe he's going inside the enclosure. If so, we might be able to slip past him. We just need to hope he doesn't spot Cora first."

In single file, they crawled through the undergrowth, back the way they had come, and further, along the perimeter of the fence. It turned out that the gate was only about a hundred metres away from where they'd been standing. While pacing back and forth, Cora must have walked past the entrance several times. It was surprising that Bauld hadn't noticed the paw prints in the muddy earth, the broken bramble stems and crushed weeds. It was pure luck that so far, he hadn't bumped into Cora.

Bauld reached the gate and was rummaging in his toolbox. When he brought out a length of steel wire and some pliers, Callum's heart plummeted. It was clear what the problem was, and it didn't look as if Bauld would need to open the gate to solve it. A piece of mesh had detached from the gatepost and was hanging loose. Bauld put his fingers through the gap, and Callum heard him curse.

"Ha! He's cut himself!" Esme couldn't keep the satisfaction out of her voice. "Serves him right, the big bully."

Then, as if Callum's prayers had been answered, Bauld took a key from his pocket and unfastened the padlock. The children watched, holding their breath, all too aware that any second now, he was going to have an unexpected encounter with Cora. Giving him a fright would have been deeply satisfying, and excellent revenge for what he'd done to Shug, but it was clear Robbie Bauld was ready to use violence and Callum feared for the lynx. Any of the objects in that toolbox could be used as a weapon.

And then Callum saw her, coming back towards them, her furry body brushing past the thorns. Cora's head kept nudging the mesh, as if, despite her encounter with the other lynx, she was still looking for a way into the enclosure. The sun's low reflection burned in her eyes, giving her a fierce, determined look. Esme gripped his sleeve. "Quick! Get the last piece of meat out of the box. You'll need it to tempt her through the gate. I'm going to distract Bauld. Good luck, Callum."

Before he could argue, Esme stood up, and ran in the opposite direction to Cora, yelling at the top of her voice. "I can't find my way back! You'll need to show me!"

Bauld looked round, eyes wide with disbelief. "Are you kiddin me? I'm no a ruddy babysitter! Find yer ain way."

Esme's voice became a high-pitched shriek.

"Well, if you don't help me find my way out, I'm going to tell my mum on you! She's a very important lawyer, you know. You'll lose your job for being horrible to poor defenceless dogs. Which way do I go? Show me!"

Bauld's face flushed. He stomped towards Esme, and

afraid for her, Callum almost followed. But if he did, he'd ruin the plan. This was their one chance. The dried meat was already in his hand, and holding Shug by the collar, staying low, he crawled towards the gate, just as Cora padded towards them.

Waving the meat with his free hand, he pushed the gate with his foot as wide as it would go and slipped inside. Without any hesitation, Cora followed. As soon as she was through the gate, she grabbed the meat out of Callum's outstretched hand and sprinted off into the trees, just as Shug wriggled out of his collar and trotted off in Cora's direction, sniffing the new smells, enjoying his freedom, oblivious to any danger.

"Shug! Come back, you daft dog!"

But it was too late. As Callum stood at the gate, wavering about what on earth to do, he saw Bauld, heading through the trees towards the lynx enclosure. They'd got Cora home, but now he and Shug were in trouble. At least Esme was safe.

12

CALLUM

At first, Callum focused only on getting out of sight, as standing on the wrong side of the gate in full view of Ross Bauld didn't seem to be the sensible option. Keeping low, he half-ran, half-crawled through the trees. Shug, crazy with excitement that one of his humans had decided to play after all, swerved between running along behind Callum, biting at his heels, and dodging in front, tripping him up.

"You really aren't helping," hissed Callum, as he hit the ground, for the second time. Shug gave the boy's nose a slobbery lick, pleased his contribution to their escape was being recognised.

Callum scrambled to his feet. There was no sign of Bauld, no sound of thudding boots or yells. It was as if he'd stepped through a portal, leaving the human world behind, and entering another. Above him, a wood warbler sang, its yellow chest so bright it looked as if it had been dipped in paint.

"Wow, Shug. Look at this place." Callum blinked in

amazement. "We're in the rainforest."

Not the Amazonian rainforest, with its trailing vines, scarlet macaws and orangutans, but the Scottish equivalent: a tiny, ancient remnant of the great swathes of temperate rainforest that had once covered Scotland's west coast. And this rainforest was just as exotic, just as strange, and dripping with as much variety of life.

For a long moment, the boy stood perfectly still, breathing in the damp, earthy scent of the forest, listening to his heartbeat drumming in his chest. With its craggy rocks and gushing waterfalls, this place felt other-worldly—like a fantasy film set—a magical forest of wood elves and unicorns. But it wasn't magical, it was real; a living reminder of Scotland's past. Weak autumn sunlight slanted through the mainly deciduous trees, a mixture of birch, ash, hazel and a few ancient, gnarled oaks. Their bark was crusted with rust-orange lichen, their leaves turning scarlet and gold. Spongy moss carpeted the soggy ground and furred the tree branches. Lush green ferns fringed white, lichen-speckled rocks. Lungwort grew in weird, cabbage-like clumps.

Shug, head down, tail sweeping the undergrowth, was totally focused on the new smells and sounds. The dog trotted along beside Callum, his paws sinking into the soft moss, snapping at the butterflies that flitted past his nose. As Callum splashed through yet another burn, half hidden by ferns and tufty grass, and squelched through boggy, black mud, he wondered how large this enclosed section of rainforest was, and how many lynx roamed among these trees.

It was the perfect environment for roe deer and smaller mammals like pine marten, red squirrels and wildcats. But because Callum knew that lynx lived here, he felt a twinge of nerves. It was all very well to know that nobody in Europe had ever been killed by a lynx in the wild, but he'd seen Cora hunt, watched the determination on her face as she focused on capturing that bird, the way her body had seemed to fly though the air.

What if a lynx is stalking us now? What if there's one on those rocks, lying in wait, preparing for an ambush?

Spooked by a strange sound, he whipped round. But it was only a wood pigeon, flapping its wings as it prepared for flight. Shug, only too happy to assist, gave chase.

"Come here! Stay close, you eejit."

Not trusting the dog to comply, Callum refastened the collar and lead. Once the lead was on, Shug dragged him along, determined as a child tugging a toboggan up the hill. Callum let himself be led. Now that he was here, in the lynx enclosure, he felt the urge to check up on Cora before they left her alone, and he hadn't a clue where to find her. Maybe, for once, Shug could help.

His sense of smell is loads better than mine. If anyone can lead me to Cora, Shug can. But, even if we find her, and it could be tricky, as she'll be virtually invisible in this forest, what next?

The uneasy feeling that he could, at any moment, be pounced on by a lynx, was making his hands so clammy with sweat that the lead was slipping through his fingers, so Callum tried to keep the thought at bay, by thinking of other things.

As a kid, I'd have loved to escape into a place like this. The thought of meeting wild animals would just have made it more exciting. It would have been a great place to build a den.

He'd built a den once, on a building site, with Robbie. It had been a good den, constructed mainly from pallets, but the security guard had sent them packing. Robbie had thought it was a brilliant joke, and had giggled uncontrollably as Callum ran, his wee brother hoiked over his shoulders like a sack of spuds.

Most of his childhood memories of Robbie were less happy ones: a snot-nosed toddler, wearing only a t-shirt and a wet, stinking nappy, whinging and clinging limpet-like to Callum in their mother's damp, cheerless flat, with its peeling wallpaper and ripped lino. He'd tried to feed Robbie crisps once, because there was no other food in the house, but his brother had spat out the crumbs, making a soggy mess on the floor, and wailed for Mum.

Stop greetin, Robbie. She'll be back soon. She's only

gone to the shops.

But Robbie didn't stop crying, and after too many evenings disturbed by the racket, the neighbours called the police, and then everything changed. After the adoption, Robbie became a different boy, living a different life. He was always smartly dressed, his hair neatly combed, his hugs stiff and awkward. For a few years, he and Robbie had seen each other every month, at soft play centres, or at McDonald's for chicken nuggets, and while it had been painful for Callum to know that in a couple of hours they'd be going their separate ways, it had also been lovely to feel he had family of his own. But then Robbie's adoptive parents had moved further away, and contact had become sporadic, and had eventually petered out. He hadn't seen his own brother for nearly two years.

Now that I'm settled, it's time that changed. I should speak to Brian or Laura about getting back in touch with him, and if they say no, I'll write to the Head of Social Work. After all, if I can do something like this, I can fight to see my wee brother. Maybe he can come and visit. I can show him round the farm… maybe he could help me make my next film…

And then Shug stopped dead, and Callum stopped thinking about Robbie, and froze too, fear almost stopping his heart. Tugging Shug's lead, pulling him backwards, Callum crouched low beside the dog, hidden behind a clump of bracken. In the dim light of the Scottish rainforest, a fully-grown lynx was approaching, padding through the undergrowth at an unhurried, relaxed pace. A female lynx by the look of it, her coat a speckled grey-brown, her fur thicker than Cora's, with long ear tufts, and wise eyes orange as a sunset. As Callum watched, fear prickling his insides, she sniffed the air, and lay down on the ground, her head resting on her huge paws, seeming oblivious to, or unbothered by, the presence of the boy and the dog crouched only a few metres away.

Callum stroked Shug's fur, hoping he'd stay calm, and out of sight.

"Good effort, lad," he whispered. "Wrong lynx, but good try."

The sound of breaking twigs made Callum jump. As another grey-brown lynx leapt from the trees, paws landing squarely on the female's back, the boy held his breath, fearing the worst. The larger female rolled over and swatted the smaller one's head with a huge paw. It took Callum a few moments to realise, this wasn't an attack; this pair were a mother and her kitten, and they were play-fighting. Shug sat stock-still at his side, seeming to realise that they were both witnessing something remarkable.

When he spotted a third lynx, coming up behind the others, Callum's heart started to pound in his chest.

Is that Cora?

This one seemed less confident, her steps slow and cautious, and as she drew nearer, it was clear he'd been right. It *was* Cora. Her coat was less glossy and luxuriant, her colouring more brown than grey, and her frame smaller and thinner than either of the other lynx. The look in her eyes was impossible to read, but her body language suggested she was nervous.

And then, without warning, Cora pounced, leaping on to the other kitten, sending him sprawling. He retaliated immediately, biting at Cora's ear tufts, swatting her tail. The female lynx pushed her way in between her squabbling kittens, nudging against them both, nuzzling them. When she began to lick Cora's fur, Callum's pulse slowed, his heart stopped racing.

A smile spread across his face. He'd never heard Cora purr, or seen that look of contentment on her face. For the first time since he'd met her—probably for the first time since Jean and Sadie had taken her away from Rothiecraig—Cora was truly happy. She'd come home, and she'd found her family.

If only Esme was here to see this. She'd be over the moon.

Pride glowed, sun-bright, in Callum's chest, as he watched the lynx family spending a few moments enjoying the last of the day's warmth, the dappled rays making their fur coats gleam. Then, without warning, the adult lynx rose and melted into the undergrowth, and as if they'd been summoned, her youngsters scrambled up and followed her. Callum ached for Cora to look back, to register his presence, but she didn't turn, and his last glimpse of the lynx was of her stubby, black-tipped tail, before she too vanished into the depths of the forest.

He turned to Shug and grinned ruefully. "She didn't even say goodbye."

In response, Shug wagged his tail and licked Callum's nose.

"Okay, I get it. You're domesticated. Cora's a wild animal. She doesn't care about us. But she does care about her family, and we've brought her home. Sadie and Jean are going to be thrilled to bits when they find out. We've done it, Shug. You, me and Esme. What a team!"

And then reality hit, like being slapped by a wet towel across the face.

How were Sadie and Jean going to find out about Cora being reunited with her family if he couldn't find his way out of the lynx enclosure? Somehow, he had to get out, right now, and he had to find Esme.

Callum stood up and ruffled Shug's ears. "Let's get moving, Shug. You did brilliantly in finding Cora. If you think you can find the way out too, now's your chance to shine."

Shug was clearly keen to get moving, but as he dragged Callum along, it appeared the dog's sense of direction was as poor as his road sense. After wasting several minutes attempting to follow Shug's meandering course, Callum gave up, and decided the best solution was to retrace their steps back to the gate where he'd left Esme.

As their boot and pawprints were imprinted in the mud this was relatively straightforward, but the return journey seemed to take ages, and when they finally reached the gate, Callum's tense shoulders sagged with relief. The sky was darkening and the prospect of being lost and alone in a pitch-black forest wasn't appealing.

"Well done, boy. You found the gate. Now all we have to do is get through it. Any clues?"

Barking, pulling on the lead, Shug jumped up at the mesh, and Callum wondered if the dog was anxious to find Esme too.

Rattling at the padlock proved useless, and the torn section of fence had been carefully repaired. Callum was bent low, considering trying to dislodge the concrete slab below the gate, when he heard a loud click. Recognising the sound, he froze.

Luka?

But when he looked up, he found himself staring into the furious face of Ross Bauld. The man held a shotgun, pointed at Callum's chest.

"What in the name of aw that's holy are you and that bloody dug doin in there?"

Bauld's voice was a roar, and Shug, recognising the

man who had kicked him, cowered behind Callum's back.

Taking a deep breath, Callum stood up straight, one palm outstretched, eyes wide and innocent. His other hand held tight to Shug's lead, in case the dog bolted back into the enclosure.

"I got locked in. Don't know how it happened. Can you let us out, please?"

There was something familiar about Bauld's mottled cheeks and red-rimmed eyes. They reminded Callum of the furious security guard who'd chased him and Robbie off the building site all those years ago. He remembered yelling, *Cannae catch a flea, you auld bampot!*

Hysterical laughter bubbled in Callum's throat, but he swallowed it down. His current situation wasn't one bit funny.

"How did you get in? What the heck are you playin at?"

Callum's mouth felt dry as sand, and when he tried to speak, no words came out. But to his relief, for the moment at least, he didn't have to explain. Without another word, Bauld dropped the shotgun into the back of his pick-up truck, and reached for the padlock, rummaging for the key. But a vein was throbbing in his neck.

He's going to let me out. But is he mad enough to shoot me or Shug?

As the padlock fell apart, Callum pushed his way past Bauld, dragging a reluctant Shug with him. Then he swung round to face the enemy. A verbal attack seemed the best form of defence.

"We could have been killed! I thought we were going to be in there all night! There are lynx in that forest you know. What were you thinking, locking us in like that? My parents will be looking everywhere for me."

As Callum ranted, Robbie Bauld stood silent, face frozen in shock. But at the mention of parents, a sneer contorted his features.

"The carpark's empty. Aw the visitors have gone home, includin your wee pal. Doesn't look like anyone's missed you at aw." His smirk morphed into a scowl. "You didn't get locked in did you? You're up to somethin."

Callum gulped, but didn't answer. Esme hadn't gone home, he was sure of that. But if Bauld thought she had, where was she hiding?

As Ross Bauld stepped towards Callum, the boy glanced to the side, seeking an escape route, and his eyes fell on a covered object, lying on the base of the pick-up next to the shotgun. The edge of the tarpaulin had been lifted at one corner, partly revealing a dead animal beneath. A sheep, its fleece snow-white, its throat uninjured. The fine hairs on the back of Callum's neck rose. He felt more uneasy out here with Bauld than he'd felt in the presence of the wild lynx.

What's Bauld doing with a dead sheep? This isn't a sheep farm and that beast isn't one of the ones we found today.

Bauld must have seen him looking because the man leant over and tugged the tarpaulin back over the corpse.

"So, confession time, son. What were you doin in that enclosure?"

Callum stayed silent, searching Bauld's face, trying to read the truth behind his bluster and aggression.

Could Bauld be responsible for killing those sheep, and making it look as though they've been savaged by wolves? And if so, how come we heard wolves howling in the night?

The boy's eyes darted to the body of the gleaming truck, with its shiny silver megaphone strapped to the top of the cab. A seed of suspicion began to root.

"It's you that's up to something." Callum spoke loudly, pretending more confidence than he felt. "Have you been driving around in the dark, playing wolf howls through that megaphone?"

Bauld didn't flinch, but a flush crept up his neck.

"What are you on about? Why the heck would I do somethin like that? The megaphone's for tellin visitors about events and to round them up at closing time. And closing time's long past. It's six o'clock. You'd better get out of here, afore I lose my temper. The side gate's unlocked. Go on. Get oot!"

As Bauld reached for the shotgun, lying in the back of

the pick-up, Callum fled. Shug raced along at his side, in as much of a hurry to escape. But before he reached the main drive, Callum stopped. His phone was in his bag, but it would be long out of charge. Somehow, he needed to let Morag Campbell know her estate manager was up to no good. Sadie and Jean would be arriving to collect them in an hour. And he had to find Esme.

13

ESME

Frances, the super-keen drama teacher who ran kids' Saturday classes in the village hall, often praised Esme's skills during freeze frame exercises and Esme was now putting all that practice to good use. As the estate manager stomped towards her, she stood stock-still, determined not to show fear. Her hands were on her hips, a scowl fixed to her face.

I am not scared. I'm angry. He works here and he should be helping me, not kicking my gran's dog. I'm not scared. I'm raging...

It was only when Bauld was so close she could smell his stale breath, that Esme bolted. Running as fast as she could, heel throbbing, she raced through the woods, desperate to give Callum time to get Cora safely into the enclosure, and keen to avoid getting caught by Ross Bauld. He'd kicked Shug, and cruelty to animals was a Very Bad Sign.

She had no idea if Bauld was coming after her, or if he'd not bothered to give chase. Her ears strained, listening for the crunch of dead leaves or crack of twigs under booted feet, but only heard the thud of her own feet and the wind whistling through the tall pines. But she couldn't be sure. For all she knew he could be getting ever closer, and fear was making her legs weak. She couldn't go on. Her blistered heels were agony, and her breath was coming in painful, wheezing gasps. Anyway, she didn't want to go any deeper into these woods. When Sadie and Gran arrived to collect them, she wanted to be with Callum and Shug at the roadside, not lost alone in a dark, spooky forest. As if to remind her she was running out of time, a tawny owl hooted, signalling that night was closing in.

Curling forward, hands on her thighs, she breathed deeply, waiting for the stitch in her side to ease. High in the trees, she could hear squirrels chattering anxiously. Maybe she was standing on one of their winter caches. Or perhaps the squirrels could hear Ross Bauld approaching. Maybe, it would best to stay just where she was, for the moment.

Swinging herself up into an ash tree, she clambered upwards and shimmied along a wide, shelf-like branch, out of sight in the tree's thick foliage.

Best thing is to wait in this tree for a while, and then head back when I'm sure the coast is clear. I should be safe enough up here.

Her thought hadn't time to take root, when it was

proved spectacularly wrong. A loud crack warned her of the danger, but the warning came far too late. Weakened by disease, the branch snapped under her weight. Screaming, Esme tumbled downwards, clutching at air.

Thudding on to the ground, she lay on her side, groaning, winded. Her shoulder ached and she guessed she'd have a big bruise later.

She'd landed on a carpet of sodden leaves and could feel dampness seeping into her trousers. A long-legged spider scuttled past her face. In the distance, the tawny owl hooted again, determined to remind her that daylight was starting to fade.

Could this day get any worse?

Esme rolled on to her back and realised it just had.

Almost invisible among the thick bushes and trees, a high mesh fence separated the fallen branch from the trunk of the ash tree.

Esme's pulse raced and she felt sick.

Please tell me I haven't fallen into the lynx enclosure!

But there was nobody around to tell her anything. She was completely alone and she had to fix this by herself. Scrambling to her feet, Esme ran to the fence, shoogling the mesh. Fear was tightening her chest, making breathing difficult, and she'd almost forgotten her painful heels and aching shoulder. A twig cracked, and her blood chilled. Her thoughts flew to the big lynx which had tried to attack Cora. Was it crouched behind her, ready to leap? Fear was making it hard to think clearly, but she had to. If she yelled, and waved her arms around, a lynx would run. She'd seen for herself how nervous they were, how alarmed by strange noises.

Esme spun round, ready to screech, but the scream died in her throat.

"Go away." The words came out as a terrified croaky whisper. The animal stood its ground, and a low, menacing growl reverberated in its throat.

As she stared into the wolf's yellow eyes, Esme's body froze, while her thoughts whirled in panicky circles. Right in front of her was the animal that had filled her childhood nightmares: the cunning, evil wolf of so many fairy tales. Esme's mouth felt dry as dust. Heart thudding against her ribs, knees trembling, she took a shaky step backwards, her foot crunching on a twig, the sleeve of her jacket snagging on brambles. The wolf's eyes were locked on hers, and she saw that his hackles had risen, and his teeth were bared. He was the Big Bad Wolf, she was Little Red Riding Hood and if her grandmother's cottage had only been in this forest, she could have run for it. But the house was miles and miles south of here and she was trapped in this enclosure. She was about to get eaten alive.

Esme heard a whimper, and knew it was hers. Her whole body was shaking now, and she hugged herself tight, trying to keep still. Panic was spiralling out of control, so she took a deep breath, sucking in oxygen, trying desperately to focus and clear her thoughts.

Think, Esme. This isn't a monster. It's a wild animal, just like Cora. What did Callum say about wolves? Real wolves, not made-up monsters?

In her head, she heard Callum's voice, and could imagine him, sitting at the campfire, stirring their pot of baked beans with a stick, talking in his quiet, gruff voice.

Esme, wolves will be more afraid of you than you are of them. Like the lynx, wolves try to steer clear of humans. Just don't look them directly in the eye. They'll feel threatened and might attack. Oh, and don't run away either, because they might see you as prey and hunt you down. Make yourself as big as you can. Wave your arms around and shout. Keep your back against a tree, as if they're in a pack, they'll try and outflank you.

She inhaled again, breathing in the sharp scent of pine. There were two things she had to do, right now: stop panicking, and stop staring at the wolf.

When she glanced around, she spotted it immediately: a possible escape route. A few metres away, a huge horse-chestnut tree stretched its limbs to the sky, its leaves a riot of green, gold, crimson and orange: its branches hopefully solid. Warily, she took a step backwards. The wolf watched her, unmoving. She took another step, and was suddenly reminded of playing *What's the Time, Mr Wolf?* at break-time in infants. Although the playground game had never been this terrifying. Her boots squelched in a muddy puddle, and the noise made her freeze, every muscle tensed. When she stole a glance at the wolf, he seemed to have moved closer.

What if he attacks? Am I close enough to the tree? If I run for it, will I reach it in time?

The truth was, she had no idea if she could outrun a wolf. Slowly, cautiously, she took another two steps back, her boots crunching now on the carpet of rotting leaves. She was almost there. Autumn sunlight shimmered through the branches of the chestnut tree, casting their shadows on the ground, faint promises of safety. But the wolf was padding towards her, long-limbed, on silent paws. She waved both arms in the air, but when she tried to yell, no sound came out. Her throat was desert-dry. The wolf stopped moving, just as he reached the leafy carpet. He made a strange noise in his throat, a cross between a growl and a bark. Esme gulped, as realisation dawned.

He's calling to the rest of the pack.

An electric current of terror zapped through her. Powered by a surge of adrenalin, she raced towards the tree, grabbed at a low branch and hauled herself upwards, ignoring the pain in her shoulder, her feet skidding on wet bark. As she climbed further up, aided by the tree's wide, solid limbs, it was like entering a welcoming haven, warmed by a fire of scarlet and amber leaves, lit by the setting sun. Esme straddled a branch, clinging on with both hands, and looked down. The wolf hadn't moved. But then an eerie, distant howl split the evening air and the wolf's ears pricked. Emboldened, he moved towards the tree, and stood on his hind legs, front paws against the tree trunk, as if contemplating the climb. For a horrible moment, Esme imagined him clambering up towards her, his jaws clamping on her ankle, dragging her back to earth.

But this was a real animal, not a mythical monster. He dropped down on to all four paws and began to circle the trunk, sniffing the ground, dog-like, reminding her of Shug. Tears trickled down her cheek when she thought of daft, sweet-natured Shug, and she let go of the branch for a second to wipe them away with her sleeve. The dog's warm furry body, snuggling up to hers, would have been a huge comfort, but it was just as well Shug hadn't been with her when the wolf had appeared. She couldn't have lifted him up into the tree, and he'd have been so excited to meet a new doggy pal, he'd have gone right up to the wolf to say hello, and probably got himself killed.

The sun had dipped below the horizon, and the darkening sky was tinged with flame. It must be almost seven o'clock. Sadie and her gran would be here soon. Perhaps they were already waiting. It was getting really cold and Esme was shivering, despite her thick jacket. If only the wolf would get tired of waiting around, she could shimmy down the tree, get on the other side of the barbed wire, find Callum and Shug and get off this estate. But the wolf wasn't showing any signs of getting bored. He was loping around the tree, rooting in the damp leaves for earthworms. In the dying light, his tawny-brown fur was fading to grey, his eyes gleaming eerily. But he was still alone. Maybe she could scare him away. Reaching out, she grabbed a thin branch and pulled one of the spiky conkers off its twig.

"Get lost, wolf! Go away!"

As she yelled, she threw the conker with all her might. It thudded onto the leaves, not even bouncing. The wolf started, glanced upwards, and then carried on circling the tree. She pulled off another conker and threw it, hard as she could, but it ricocheted off a lower branch and plopped on to the ground. Desperation making her heart race, Esme looked around, but no other conkers were nearby. A few hung in spiky clusters from the highest branches, but she couldn't risk a climb. Most of the conkers had fallen naturally, and were lying on the ground, split and rotting and useless as weapons. When she pulled at a thin branch and it snapped off in her hand, fear stirred in her stomach.

Is this tree dying too? Could the branch I'm sitting on break as easily as this one?

But she did her best with the stick, aiming it straight at the wolf's body, just as he stepped back into the shadows. The branch thwacked on to the ground and the wolf moved forwards again and sniffed, more curious than alarmed. Shug would have grabbed the stick and bounded off, body wriggling with excitement. This wolf didn't appear remotely interested in playing fetch.

Esme pulled at another thin branch, but this one was more pliable, and no matter how hard she tugged and twisted it she was unable to break it off. She was beginning to lose hope. Looking down, Esme saw that the wolf was now standing right beneath her, his great head arched back, his nose pointing towards the purple-tinged evening sky, and its pale sliver of rising moon. And then the wolf howled. The eerie, ominous sound echoed through the woods, and sent a shiver of fear coursing up her spine.

Clinging to the branch, with all four limbs, like a koala to a eucalyptus, she tried to slow her breathing, but terror was making her heart pound. Because the other wolves were coming on command, grey as shadows, slipping ghost-like from the cover of the trees. One member of the pack padded straight towards the big chestnut tree, and paced around the foot, sniffing at the air, aware of an unfamiliar presence in their midst.

How have I ended up here? I'm supposed to be getting ready for Isobel's party, putting on the sparkly top I bought in Inverness months ago, when we were still friends. I should be painting my nails with glittery varnish, gelling my hair into spikes. Instead, I'm trapped in a waking nightmare. What if lose my grip and fall to the ground again and get ripped to shreds by the wolfpack? What if...?

Panic rose in her throat again, and she choked on a scream.

Calm down, you eejit. Panicking won't help. And I won't lose my grip. I'll stay up here until the wolves leave or until help comes. It'll be okay. Even if I fall, they might get such a fright they'll run away. Remember what Callum said, that they try and avoid humans, because they know how dangerous we are. Let's face it, I'm probably safer up here than I would have been at Isobel's party. If I'd turned up tonight, after everything that's happened between us, she'd have been horrible to me. In front of everyone, she'd have made fun of my hair, my clothes, my voice...

For some reason, the thought calmed her. She wasn't going to the party and didn't have to face Isobel tonight. She was safe enough up here in the tree. Eventually, hopefully, the wolves would move on, or return to their den. And then she'd find Callum and Shug and they'd go home, and have hot cocoa and buttered toast in her gran's house, and Sadie and Gran would listen, open mouthed while she and Callum told them about their adventures.

And when I get back to school, I'll tell Isobel we're over. I'll say sorry to all the kids I've been mean to. I'll start over... OMG, how cute are those?

The wolf at the foot of the tree had been joined by three fluffy cubs, playful as puppies, scrambling over each other, play-fighting. The mother wolf glanced upwards, a wary look in her eyes and moved away from the tree, followed by the cubs.

Esme wanted to call to her, tell her not to be afraid, she wouldn't hurt her babies. Instead, she watched the cubs as they moved towards the trees, stalking each other, pouncing, practising the hunting skills they'd use in later life, and some of her fear of the wolves seeped away.

These were wild animals, who'd been trying to get on with their lives in the wilderness, without interference by humans. They'd been brought here and fenced in, used in an experiment. If the experiment had failed, if these wolves *were* killing sheep, it wasn't their fault.

The alpha wolf, who'd been patrolling the edge of the clearing, stopped and raised his head, as if he'd heard a noise. Esme listened too but could hear nothing. But then she jerked upright, so sharply she almost toppled off her branch. From somewhere in the dark distance, Callum was calling her name. A gruff, familiar bark told her Shug was with him. One hand flew to her mouth, stifling a scream. But she had to let Callum know about the wolves. She couldn't hide up here and watch him and Shug get hurt.

The dog barked again, loud and excited, and a sob

broke from her throat. Somehow, Callum and Shug must have entered the wolves' enclosure too, and they were in terrible danger.

"Wolves!" she screamed, heart crashing against her ribs. "Wolves! Get out of here!"

14

ESME

Her brain was conjuring up horrible images: Shug being attacked, throat ripped open, like those poor ewes, Callum running for his life, pursued by the pack. But her eyes were telling her a different story. On silent paws, the wolves were slipping away. The mother lifted the smallest cub by the scruff of its neck, and carried it out of the clearing, the other youngsters scrambling after them. Esme caught a last glimpse of ghost-grey fur, as the pack melted into the trees. The wolves were achieving something she and Callum had failed to do in the last few days—avoid trouble and stay out of danger.

Callum's torch beam was circling the clearing, spotlighting one tree and then another. When the beam landed on Esme, she blinked, half-blinded, and straightened up, not wanting him to know she'd been cowering, terrified.

"There you are! We've been looking everywhere for you! How the heck did you get in there?"

As her eyes adjusted, Esme could see Callum waving

at her, a dark silhouette in the gathering twilight, and the truth dawned. Callum and Shug were on the other side of the fence, outside of the wolves' enclosure. They'd never been in danger from the wolf pack. And then she realised that Callum wasn't just waving, he was gesturing towards a higher branch.

"Climb along that branch, Esme, and then you can drop down on the other side."

When she looked up, Esme realised he'd been pointing to the branch laden with conkers, the one she'd felt too afraid to climb up to earlier. Even now, when the wolves were no longer patrolling underneath, her nerves twanged at the prospect of the climb. A fall from a tree and a close encounter with a wolf seemed more than enough drama for one evening. But the alternative, staying where she was, felt much scarier.

I can do this. I have to, or I'm going to have to spend all night in the wolves' enclosure. I'll miss my chance to head home tonight with Gran. My chance to eat a decent meal, and to have a warm bubble bath and hot chocolate with marshmallows, and to sleep in a comfy bed and eat eggy soldiers in the morning... and to use a flushing loo.

Once she'd begun to climb, her confidence grew. As long as she didn't look down, it was just like clambering on the climbing wall at the sports centre. The hard part was the final section. Only the very tip of the branch overhung the fence, so she had to edge all the way along it, feeling the increasingly slender branch bend under her weight, terrified it would snap as the ash branch had done. She'd almost reached the end, only a metre left to go, when she heard a small crack. Petrified she was going to fall back down into the wolves' enclosure, Esme edged a little further, eyes squeezed shut, hands clammy with fear.

"You're nearly there. Another metre!"

Callum sounded confident, his words reassuring, and when Esme opened her eyes she saw he was right. Her legs were dangling directly above the fence, her feet almost touching the mesh. But the branch was now skinny and pliable, and as she shimmied forward, it started to bend even further, until she was in real danger of sliding off. Terrified she was going to end up on the wrong side of the fence, Esme flung herself, arching like a pole vaulter across the mesh. As she crashed head-first through a straggly bramble bush, scratching her cheek, ripping her jacket, a feeling of triumph surged through her veins and anaesthetised the pain.

I've done it! I've escaped!

Shug bounded towards her, and spun on the spot, giddy with excitement, his wagging tail sweeping across her face. He barked furiously, delighted with himself, as if Esme had been playing a game of hide and seek and he'd been terribly clever in finding her.

"Calm down, Shug. Let me untangle myself first, and

I'll give you a big hug."

A flash of light gave away Callum's approach.

"What happened? How did you end up in there? Are you okay?"

She opened her mouth and a single word came out, instead of the sentence in her head.

"Wolves…"

Callum shone the torch through the fence, sweeping the beam across the empty clearing.

"I can't see any. Did you hear them howling?"

Annoyance made her voice scratchy. "They were there. Believe me. You and Shug were so loud you scared them away."

"Oh, wow. Amazing. How many did you see?"

"Callum, I wasn't filming for a wildlife programme. The wolves found me, not the other way round. Why the heck do you think I was up that tree?" She sat down on a tree stump, suddenly dizzy. "I was surrounded by the whole pack. It was very, very scary."

The torch swung back to her face. He must have seen something in her expression, because his tone changed. "It must have been scary, especially when it's getting so dark. I'm glad you're alright." He was grinning, crooked teeth gleaming white in the torchlight. "I need to tell you some brilliant news. Cora has found her mum, and her wee sister. She looked so happy, Esme. I wish you'd seen her."

The tight knot of fear had already loosened, and the emotion in Callum's voice unravelled her.

Cora's home. I did it, Gran.

Whooping, Esme punched the air, hardly caring how she looked, although whether she'd have done it in broad daylight, or in front of Isobel, was another matter entirely.

"We did it, Cal!"

His grin widened. "Yeah, we did, didn't we? You, me and Shug the Dug… The Rewilders." He swung his torch so the beam lit up the rows of pine trees. "But we'd better get out of here. I don't want to bump into Ross Bauld, especially now he knows I've figured out what he's up to."

"What do you mean? What *is* he up to?"

"It was you that put the idea in my head, that someone has been trying to sabotage the rewilding experiment. But I'm pretty sure it isn't Luka and his grandfather who are responsible for those sheep carcasses. I think it's Ross Bauld. He doesn't want the wild animals on the estate and he's hoping to stir up opposition among the locals. He's only pretending to support Morag Campbell and her work." Callum paused. "The trouble is, I don't have any hard evidence, so I don't think there's much we can do. Once we get picked up, we can let Sadie know and she'll tell the Rydeskis."

"So, we should just focus on getting to the car." Esme pulled a snaking bramble stem from around her ankle.

"Let's go."

It was a long, long way back through the pine woods to the main gate and Esme felt every minute tick past. It was clear they were going to be well over an hour late, and by now, the only thing she wanted was to be squeezed into the front cab of Sadie's pick-up, feeling the heater blast in her face, knowing she was heading home to her gran's house.

The tawny owls' hoots were eerie in the darkness. When she looked up, through the trees' dying foliage, she glimpsed the crescent moon, delicate as a bracelet charm, nestled on star-sequinned black velvet, and she thought again of Isobel's party.

Beyond the next line of trees, the lights of the gatehouse cottage shone. As they crept past, towards the main gate, Esme spotted Bauld inside, sitting in an armchair in front of the telly, and felt comforted, knowing they weren't being followed.

But when they walked towards the main gate, it dawned on her that they *were* being followed, after all. Behind her, boots were crunching on gravel, and she was sure she could hear someone breathing.

Turning sharply, she hissed. "Who's there?"

A figure stepped out of the shadows, giving Shug such a fright he almost leapt into Esme's arms, and then tried to redeem himself by barking furiously.

"Hush, Shug!" hissed Callum. "Hi, Luka. What are

you doing, sneaking about in the dark?"

"I could ask you the same thing." Luka's face was moon-pale in the darkness. "Look, I owe you two an apology. I've figured it out. It's Bauld who's responsible for killing the sheep."

"We know," sighed Callum. "But we don't have any proof."

Satisfaction glowed in Luka's voice. "I do."

Taking a deep breath, his explanation rushed out in a torrent.

"When Grandpa and me were here earlier this evening, I uncovered a dead sheep in the back of Bauld's pick-up. It was marked as belonging to the croft at Ailcraggan, and Bauld had no good reason I could think of for having it in his van, so it made me suspicious. I started to wonder if the dead sheep we'd found had been left there by him. And then I guessed maybe he'd shot them, let his dog loose on the bodies and then left the mutilated corpses for the farmers to find, knowing they'd blame the wolves."

"That's what we figured." When Callum spoke, Esme felt her shoulders sag with relief that he didn't mention her first theory. "But I can't think why he'd do such a thing. Apparently, he tells everyone he's the project's main supporter."

Luka gave a bitter laugh. "He's a dirty liar. While he was speaking to my grandpa in the cottage, I asked to use the toilet, and sneaked into his study. His laptop was open and I had a wee look through his recent emails. The two-faced git is taking handouts from a big organisation, one that makes their money through developing land for housing. As you can imagine, they're dead keen to prevent rewilding in Scotland."

"It's a lot of bother to go to for a handout." Callum didn't sound convinced.

"There's a lot of money involved, and he's prepared to go further. According to the emails I saw, if Plan A doesn't work, Plan B is to poison any lynx kits and wolf cubs being born on the estate, to ensure the project can't continue for long." Luka grimaced. "I could hardly believe what I was reading. I mean, I'm no a fan of rewilding, but this guy's out of order."

Esme's thoughts flew to Cora, and her sister, and the wolf cubs. "That's terrible. He's evil. We need to stop him!"

"Done." Luka's tone was a wee bit smug. "I told my grandpa what I'd discovered and we waited outside the gates until dark, and then I sneaked back in, so Bauld wouldn't see the pick-up heading for the big house, realise we were on to him, an decide to destroy the evidence. I've told Lady Campbell it aw and the police are on their way. My grandfather's waiting outside the gates."

"Your grandpa's probably telling Sadie everything."

Callum grinned. "Hopefully, she's out there too, waiting for Esme and me." He shone his torch down the drive. "We'd better get out of here. Shug's barking was pretty loud, and it's possible Bauld heard it."

They hurried to the main gate and were a few metres away when Luka spoke.

"The only other thing that's worrying me is that Grandpa and me heard a wolf howling, two nights in a row, so is it possible that one *has* escaped?"

A shiver of fear ran up Esme's spine at the prospect of meeting another wolf, but Callum gave a bitter laugh.

"No, I reckon Bauld has been playing tricks on us. I think he has been travelling about in his van at night, playing recordings of wolf howls through the megaphone." He paused.

"In fact, I'd take a bet on it. There was red dirt all over the wheel rims, and I'm pretty sure that would have come from Glen Craig."

"Well, well, well – if it isn't those meddling kids and their daft mutt!" The voice in the darkness was mocking. "Do you think you're in some kids' cartoon on the telly or something? Your dug's no got a scooby, that's for sure!"

Callum swung his torch in the direction of the voice and Bauld stepped out from behind a tree. In the torchlight, the man's cheeks were blotchy, his nose a web of broken veins, his eyes as cold as a shark's.

He was holding a shotgun, and when he laughed, the

barrel jiggled up and down.

"I figured we had burglars. Nearly shot you deid."

Shug whined, and tucked his body behind Esme's, so close she could feel his body shivering. Callum let go of the dog's lead.

"Hold onto Shug," he whispered.

"Oi, put that thing down. Don't even think about it!" Bauld's body twisted, aiming the shotgun at Luka, and the boy let his air rifle drop.

"The police are on their way!" Luka's voice was a terrified croak.

Bauld sighed, as if they'd all let him down badly. "Well, that's a shame. But luckily, when the polis come, you three weans are goin to tell them you've made up a pack of lies."

"We will not." Esme stepped forward, trying to ignore the tremble in her voice. "We'll tell the police the whole truth."

As the shotgun swung towards her, her legs turned to liquid and Shug growled, low in his throat, a ferocious snarl Esme had never heard him make before.

As if he'd been transformed, docile pet to wild beast, Shug flew at Bauld. Snarling, teeth bared like a wolf's, the dog pounced, sinking his canines into Bauld's arm, and shaking his prey like a rat.

Bauld yelled, and tried to free himself, whipping his arm forwards and backwards, kicking out at Shug. The dog yelped, but hung on, jaws clamped tight, grimly determined.

And then the gun went off, the blast so loud, Esme yelled in fright. She, Callum and Luka threw themselves to the ground, and curled up, hands over their heads, while a terrible, animal scream ripped the night. It went on, and on, a high-pitched, ghastly sound, and then stopped, dead. The sudden silence was unnerving.

Cautiously, Esme raised her head. "Shug?" Her whisper rose to a wail. "Shug?"

Something was happening at the gate. A police officer was cutting the padlock, spot-lit by a car's headlights. As the officer opened the gate, the car shot forwards, siren blasting, piercing the quiet. Its flashing blue light revealed a terrible scene. Bauld was slumped against a tree, thrown backwards by the force of the blast. His face was ghost-white, his features a distorted mask of agony. A dark pool of blood was forming round his mangled boot.

"He's literally shot himself in the foot," growled Luka. "Serves the bampot right."

Another police officer had got out the car, and Esme could see two more figures hurrying through the gate... Jan Rydeski and Sadie McIvor. But there was no sign of Shug.

Ignoring the commotion going on around her, Esme grabbed Callum's torch and started checking under bushes, behind trees, calling Shug's name. Her chest felt so tight it was hard to breathe, and she was almost too scared to look, terrified she'd find him lying, limp and lifeless.

Callum came over, put his hand on her arm.

"The police want to speak to you, Esme. Go and have a word with them. I'll find Shug. I promise."

Tears pouring down her cheeks, feeling as if she was living through a nightmare, she nodded, and walked over to tell the police what she knew about Bauld's crimes. But every time she thought of how brave Shug had been, how wild and fierce and protective, her voice broke and she felt another piece of her heart shatter.

Sadie McIvor's sharp tone cut through the darkness like a knife.

"The lassie's had enough for one night. I'm taking her home. No don't bother arguing wi me. You two can come and speak to her in the morn." Without waiting for their agreement, Sadie steered Esme away from the police, and led her towards the gate, standing back briefly to let an ambulance enter. "Callum!" she yelled. "Come on, son. It's time to go home."

As Callum walked towards them, blinking in the glare of the ambulance's lights, Esme's heart leapt. The boy was weighed down by a heavy, wriggling bundle of fur in his arms.

"Shug! Oh, Shug!"

Half-blinded by tears, heart brimming with joy, Esme ran, and threw her arms around the dog, held firmly in Callum's arms. She felt so grateful to Callum that she didn't care that she was hugging the boy as tightly as the dog.

"I found him behind the gatehouse, going through the bins. Greedy beast. No, Shug, you're not having the rest of that mingin chicken. We're going home. Aren't we, Esme?"

Esme nodded, not trusting herself to speak. Shug's breath smelled vile, but she didn't care.

"Come on, lass. He's right as rain." Sadie's voice was uncharacteristically gentle. "It's time to go."

Callum retrieved their backpacks, and as Esme hoiked hers on to her sore shoulders, she felt overwhelmed, and had to bite her lip to stop more tears from falling. Her entire body ached, but her heart was singing.

Sadie's pick-up was a few hundred metres from the gate, parked right beside Jan Rydeski's. She didn't say any more as they clambered in, except to comment that they were both in dire need of a good wash.

"You can tell us aw aboot your adventures when we get to Jean's. She's made steak pie wi mountains of mash and apple crumble and custard, so I hope you're baith hungry.'

Esme's mouth began to water at the prospect of a decent meal. Shug squeezed in beside them in the front cab. His breath still smelled icky, but his warmth and weight were comforting. She put her arms round him and hugged him tight.

"You're a hero, Shug," she whispered.

"Wasn't he just? What a guy. And us too. The Rewilders are freaking heroes."

There was a smile in Callum's voice that warmed her insides, and, weirdly, made her want to burst into tears. Because he was right. Together, she and Callum and Shug had done something heroic. Cora was back with her mother, a wild lynx once more, free to live independently in the forest.

Esme knew her gran was going to be thrilled by the news, and massively proud of her. If she was being honest, she was super proud of herself. She didn't even regret her terrifying time in the wolves' enclosure. Not many people could say they'd encountered a pack of wolves in the almost-wild.

Her only regret was that she'd been so mean to Callum at school, because when their temporary truce ended, she was going to be the loneliest girl in the world.

15

CALLUM

As Sadie's pick-up rumbled through the village, they passed Isobel's house on Main Street. The big, wrought-iron gate was festooned with pink and silver balloons, and the DJ's music was booming from an open window. The living room curtains were open, and through the condensation on the glass, Callum could see the room was crowded, a blur of colour, noise and excitement.

He gazed at the house, half-expecting to feel twinges of envy, and anger, that he'd been excluded, but the feelings didn't come.

I've been in a rainforest and met a lynx and her cubs. I win.

Callum glanced at Esme but couldn't read the expression on her face.

He kept his voice low. "It's not too late. You could still go. Are you sure you don't want me to ask Sadie to drop you off?"

"No, I'm not dressed, am I?" Esme sighed heavily. "To tell the truth, I don't think I'd be welcome, and even if

I was, I really don't want to go. Isobel and I have had a major fall out. We're not friends anymore." She paused, as though she was thinking it over. "I'm not sure we've ever been friends, really. When I go back to school, I'm hoping her nasty remarks won't hurt one bit, because I'm not interested in trying to hold on to a friendship that isn't real. For the first time in forever, I feel free to be me. Sorry if none of that makes any sense. I'm a bit tired."

She didn't look at Callum while she spoke, just stared out of the window, and kept her face averted as they left the village and headed in the direction of Jean's house. He was trying really hard to think of something kind to say, something that would help, but everything he came up with seemed fake.

There was no point in him lying, pretending he was sorry she and Isobel had fallen out. And what could he say about the nasty remarks? Of course they'd hurt, because Esme hadn't had time to grow a hard shell, or to develop a couldn't-care-less attitude. He knew exactly how she'd feel, and if he'd been asked last week, he'd have said being on the receiving end of bullying would serve Esme McKinnon right.

They were almost at her grandmother's cottage before she spoke again.

"If I've learned anything recently, it's that real friends have your back. With a real friend, you can be yourself. I don't even like the person I pretend to be when I'm with Isobel." She fell silent and when she continued, her voice sounded choked. "I don't think anybody likes that person much. So, things need to change."

Seeming to sense her sadness, Shug burrowed his furry head into Esme's neck, and licked her chin.

"Don't, Shug. That's gross." But Callum noticed that she didn't push the dog away, just held him tighter.

He cleared his throat. "When school starts back, you and me can reinstate open warfare, if you like. Or we could continue the truce." He paused, unsure if he should continue, wondering if he was being stupid to trust her, when Shug gave him a slobbery lick, as if he was trying to communicate something important.

She's brave. She's funny. She saved your life.

Callum took a deep breath.

"Alternatively, and this is my preferred option, we could declare a permanent ceasefire. Be friends, even."

Sadie swerved the pick-up down the lane, and in the glow of Jean's outside light, Callum saw the beaming smile on Esme's face, the happiness sparkling in her eyes.

"I'd love to be friends. I mean, I'd need to overlook the fact you're a right know-it-all, but I think it could work."

"Yeah, well, I'll need to overlook the weird way you eat a sandwich. That nibbling the crusts thing is so ruddy annoying."

Callum flung open the car door. Thrilled to be home, Shug leapt from the vehicle as if he'd been shot from a catapult and raced round the front garden, only stopping to pee on the grass.

The front door opened. Esme's gran stood on the step, arms spread in greeting.

"You did it, didn't you? I kent you would! You wee superstars!"

Shug leapt up, scraping his claws against her legs, delighted his bravery was being recognised. Clicking her tongue in irritation, Jean pushed him down.

"No you, you eejit. I bet you've been a liability. Esme… my best girl! Come in! You must be starving!"

Callum and Sadie shuffled past, leaving Esme and her gran hugging at the door. As he breathed in the warm cooking smells, his stomach rumbled.

Jean's living room had been aired and scrubbed and smelled fresh again. The room was cluttered but tidy, the worst of the damage cleared away. The deep gouges in the wallpaper and scratch marks on the wooden furniture were the only evidence that this had once been home to a lynx.

Callum closed his eyes, picturing Cora full-size, stalking roe deer in the ancient rainforest, disturbing the peace, moving the deer herds around, so trees could survive. Perhaps in time she'd have kittens of her own, and perhaps one day, they'd be released to roam where they pleased. He, Esme, Luka and Shug had given the lynx a chance.

Behind him, Sadie spoke, making him jump. "It's been awfy hard, the last few days."

"Yeah, but she had to go. And at least Jean's house doesn't stink of cat pee anymore."

Sadie's face twisted, as if she was going to cry. "I'm no talking about the lynx, you daft lummox! Aye, I missed Cora too, but if you'd brought her back, Jean and I would have been devastated." She ruffled his hair. "It was you I missed. Couldn't be doing wi the quiet. And I couldn't be prouder of you, son. It'll be great to have you home for guid."

16

ESME

When Esme woke the next morning, the bed sheets were twisted in a knot, from the tossing and turning she'd been doing all night, and her head was dull and fuzzy. It felt as if she'd spent the whole night fleeing monsters, falling from cliffs, hunting for lost loved ones. Pushing off the patchwork quilt, she dressed, splashing cold water on her face from the old-fashioned washstand.

When she went into the kitchen, her gran took one look at her and ushered her through to the living room.

"You look shattered, lass. Go and have a wee lie down on the couch and I'll make you some porridge."

So, she went straight from bed to couch, where she lay most of the day, aching legs covered by a crocheted blanket, while Shug snored in front of the wood-burning stove. Being treated like a Victorian invalid felt rather nice, and she felt sad that it would be over soon.

School's going to be awful tomorrow. I told Callum I wouldn't care if Isobel's horrible, but that was a big fat lie.

"No wonder you're exhausted, lass, after aw that

walking and aw that drama." Her gran bustled into the living room, carrying a tray. "Here's a wee bite of lunch. Lentil soup and crusty bread. There's cranachan for pudding."

Still a bit full after mid-morning scones and strawberry jam, Esme leant against the pile of cushions and gave her gran a cheeky grin. "Are you feeling a wee bit guilty, Gran, by any chance?"

Her gran stuck out her tongue. "No even a wee bit. It's aw turned out very well, if you ask me." Plonking the tray down on the pine trunk, she stuck a hand in her cardigan pocket. "Oh, here's your phone. It has beeped a few times." She headed towards the door, and then turned. "Sadie was right about something, at least. That Callum's a guid lad."

Before tucking into the soup, Esme checked her phone. There were three unread messages and her first instinct was to delete them all, convinced they'd be from Isobel. But the urge to check was too strong.

When she did, she felt her shoulders sag with relief. None of the messages were from Isobel. The first was from Mum, in reply to Esme's last text.

Love you too, sweetie. See you soon. xxxx

Then another from Mum, sent an hour ago.

Boarding shortly. Home by dinner time. I'll make it up to you next weekend. Cinema and shopping trip to Inverness? Xxx

The third was from Callum, sent ten minutes earlier. *Hi Esme, Got your number from your gran. I took this in Glen Craig and I thought you might like it as a souvenir. Hope Shug survived his chicken dinner. See you tomorrow. Cal*

Her first feeling was annoyance. *All that time Callum had his phone with him… and Gran wouldn't let me take mine!*

But then she looked at the video clip Callum had sent and the annoyance melted.

It was a stunningly beautiful scene, a warm, glowing medley of autumn colours. Sunlight glanced through russet leaves, glimmering on a long-limbed lynx with brilliant amber eyes and a girl with gleaming auburn hair. As the animal approached to take food from her outstretched hand, the girl's smile widened and her eyes sparkled with happiness.

Esme paused the film and stared at the girl's joy-filled face.

This is the me I want to be.

Before switching off her phone, Esme sent a reply.

Thanks. I love it. See you tomorrow. Sit next to you in English? E

THE END

GLOSSARY

Aboot—about

Ain—own

Auld—old

Aw—all

Awfy—quite

Awright—alright

Baith—both

Bampot—an idiot

Besom—insulting word for girl or woman (can also be used affectionately)

Bunnet—a hat or bonnet

Cannae—can't

Cranachan—a Scottish dessert made with oats, raspberries, cream and whisky

Deid—dead

Dreich—miserable (often describes the weather)

Dug—a dog

Eejit—an idiot

Gawp—to stare

Gowping—throbbing painfully

Greetin—crying

Guid—good

Heid—head

Heidie—Head Teacher

Hoodie crow—a hooded crow

Hoose—a house

Hoik—to pull something up

Kent—knew

Lochan—a small loch or lake

Lummox—a clumsy or stupid person

Mair—more

Manky—dirty and unpleasant

Mingin—disgusting

No—not

Numpty—a stupid person

Och—Oh!

Oot—out

Polis—the Police

Roon—round

Rammy—a fight or argument

Saltire—the Scottish flag

Scooby—a clue (from Scooby-Doo)

Smirr—fine rain or drizzle

Stramash—an uproar or a disturbance

Shoogle—to shake something

Tellt—told

Wi—with

Weans—children

Wheesht!—Be quiet!

Wummin—woman

Yin—one

Yer—your

Yoursels—yourselves

AUTHOR'S NOTE

Scotland was once a country of enormous forests, peat bogs and wetlands, where wolves, bears and lynx roamed freely. But much of the land's biodiversity has been lost and the large predators are long gone, hunted to extinction by farmers afraid for their livestock and by hunters for fur and sport.

In recent years, the idea of reintroducing wolves and lynx has been raised, as a way of keeping deer on the move, helping to prevent overgrazing and damage to tree saplings. Some people are appalled by the prospect and in *The Rewilders*, I've tried to show that the different points of view are valid and need to be listened to and respected. Compromise and consensus will be necessary if large predators are ever going to be successfully reintroduced.

I fully appreciate that the aims of Rewilding Scotland are about so much more than the reintroduction of large mammals. Their goal is *"a flourishing ecosystem, supporting self-sustaining nature-based economies which secure a future for local communities."* The hope is that by planting native trees and reviving damaged peatlands, Scotland's biodiversity will increase and natural processes will be revived. Scotland's fragments of temperate rainforest, in which a section of *The Rewilders* is set, are internationally important and contain the world's rarest bryophytes and lichens.

But lynx are stunningly beautiful animals and the prospect of reintroducing them to the Highlands gets people excited, so I'm not going to apologise for putting lynx rather than lichen at the centre of my novel. My hope is that young people read *The Rewilders* and are inspired to discover more about the rewilding movement. Whether or not wolves and lynx ever return to Scotland, action is needed now to bring our natural world back to life.

Lindsay Littleson
x

ACKNOWLEDGEMENTS

With grateful thanks to:

Anne Glennie at Cranachan Books, for all her enthusiasm and hard work. I feel so lucky to be writing for such a fabulous small publisher!

All of the Clan Cranachan authors. Their support and excellent chat have been so important to me, particularly during these challenging times.

The Scottish Rewilding Alliance. Their live webinar was brilliant and their collaborative approach has got to be the way forward.

David Hetherington, whose book, *The Lynx and Us*, was a fabulous source of information and inspiration. The fascinating facts and beautiful photos made it impossible not to fall under the spell of the lynx.

Jacquelyn Else-Jack and Andrew Givan of Children's Libraries in Renfrewshire, for continuing to be so supportive of local authors. Libraries rock!

Teachers Ann McInnes and Alan Hepburn for offering advice and information about useful contacts and websites.

My partner Ian, who puts up with my constant whinging and rarely complains.

My lovely family. Love you all to bits. xx

ABOUT THE AUTHOR

Lindsay Littleson lives with her partner Ian and their very noisy cat in Uplawmoor, a small village near Glasgow. Lindsay is an ex-primary teacher who now writes full-time, when she is not drinking tea and eating chocolate biscuits (both remarkably time-consuming activities).

She began writing for children in 2014 and won the Kelpies Prize for her first children's novel *The Mixed-Up Summer of Lily McLean*. The sequel, *The Awkward Autumn of Lily McLean*, was published by Floris Books in 2017. *Guardians of the Wild Unicorns* came out in 2019 and was nominated for the 2020 CILIP Carnegie Medal. Her latest novel with Floris, *Secrets of the Last Merfolk*, came out in summer 2021.

In 2015 her WW1 novel *Shell Hole* was shortlisted for the Dundee Great War Children's Book Prize and she enjoyed engaging in research so much that she was inspired to write another two historical books, *A Pattern of Secrets*, set in Victorian Paisley, and *The Titanic Detective Agency*. *The Rewilders*, published by Cranachan, is Lindsay's seventh children's novel.

Website: lindsaylittleson.co.uk
Twitter: @ljlittleson
Instagram: @lindsaylittleson